William Chambers

My Holidays

William Chambers

My Holidays

ISBN/EAN: 9783337287443

Printed in Europe, USA, Canada, Australia, Japan

Cover: Foto ©Andreas Hilbeck / pixelio.de

More available books at **www.hansebooks.com**

MY HOLIDAYS

BY

The Right Hon. WILLIAM CHAMBERS

OF GLENORMISTON

LORD PROVOST OF EDINBURGH

PRINTED FOR PRIVATE CIRCULATION

1867

THE following Sketches refer to my Excursions as a Commissioner of Northern Light-houses along the coasts of Scotland in 1866 and 1867. Written for amusement, at intervals of leisure after returning home, and printed in this form as a gift to a few private friends, the Sketches, however imperfect, may possibly convey an idea of one of the many duties assigned to the office which I have at present the honour to occupy.

W. C.

September 1867.

MY FIRST HOLIDAY.

AN amusing peculiarity in the office of the Lord Provost of Edinburgh is the obligation of being a member of so many public bodies, that he would frequently have to give his presence at five or six places at precisely the same hour—a thing not easily done, even with the aid of a carriage and pair of horses. In circumstances of this perplexing nature, his Lordship usually compounds with his sense of duty—sometimes preferring one Board, and sometimes another, with perhaps a kind of leaning to some one in particular. In occupying the onerous position here referred to, if I have had any preference at all, it has been for the Commission of Northern Light-houses, a body invested with the duty of managing all the light-houses on the sea-coast of Scotland and Isle of Man, now amounting to nearly sixty in number (to say nothing of buoys and beacons), and involving an expenditure of eight-and-twenty thousand pounds per annum.

This Northern Commission may be accepted as a fair specimen of that little understood state of affairs in which many people, for the honour of the thing, give their time and trouble for nothing—certainly nothing in the way of cash. A story is told of Joseph Hume having, in his virtuous indignation in parliament, described the Commission of northern luminaries as being a regular and costly job, when he was set right by the Lord Advocate of the day, who stated that the whole remuneration derived by the Commissioners for their trouble consisted in a dinner once a year—whereupon Joseph, in a state of munificent repentance, declared that they should in future have two dinners instead of one! These two dinners are now, accordingly, a settled institution in Edinburgh, the head-quarters of the Commission ; and, from experience, I can say that the institution is conducted in no niggard fashion. Supposing the story to be correct, the Lord Advocate might have added, that half-a-dozen or so of the Commissioners, along with two or three guests, are indulged with an excursion, free of expense, annually in the *Pharos*, a powerful and commodious paddle-steamer belonging to the Board, which is employed in carrying stores to, and in making periodical inspections of, the several light-houses.

Who is to go in the *Pharos* is sometimes a matter of delicate consideration. The Commissioners consist of certain crown-officers, and sheriffs of maritime counties, along with some civic magistrates ; and at a meeting for the purpose, the selection is properly adjusted, not a little depending on the wish of the parties, for what some may consider to be a privilege, others view as a positively irksome or impracticable duty. In 1866, my first year of office, I was honoured by being named one of the excursionists ; and not disinclined to a little airy variety in the routine of public business, I ventured to give my assent. The only real pinch was how to get away. The *Pharos* was to depart for its voyage on the west coast on the 23d of July, but owing to certain civic matters of pressing concern, I could not leave for some days later ; by these means, I lost the Clyde, Galloway, and Isle of Man part of the excursion, and had to be taken up in the harbour of Belfast, where the *Pharos* was appointed to lie tranquilly during Sunday the 29th.

Apropos of the Isle of Man—what has it to do with the Northern Commission ? Thereby hangs a tale. Light-houses, as is very reasonable, are supported from the proceeds of statutory dues payable by the ships which are presumed to benefit by them—outgoing foreign vessels paying the dues on starting, and vessels entering port paying on arrival—the whole managed in a neat way by the officers of customs. In old times—say fifty years ago—the Isle of Man had its own system of lights, which were so bad as to be complained of by the Liverpool traders ; and it became obvious that these lights should pass under the authority of one of the three Boards of the United Kingdom—the Trinity House of England, the Ballast Board of Ireland, or the Northern Lights of Scotland. The method adopted for settling the question was exceedingly rational ; it was to ask what each Board would take to light the Isle of Man, and adopt that which was cheapest. The Trinity offered to maintain the lights for twopence per ton on all vessels that passed ; while the Northern Commission declared its readiness to accept the very small sum of a farthing per ton. This was in 1815, since which time the Isle of Man, in the matter of light-houses, has been connected with Scotland. The farthing per ton was a shrewd conception. So large is the number of vessels passing the Isle of Man, that this forms the best-paying branch of revenue of the Northern Lights.

Reaching Belfast (by way of Greenock) early on the morning of Saturday 28th, and hospitably entertained and escorted about by an esteemed citizen, I had an opportunity of visiting the more remarkable places in the town and neighbourhood, and learning some particulars worthy of note. As it was twenty years since I had seen Belfast, I was not prepared for its vast extension and numerous street improvements, or for learning that the annual income of its harbour has risen, since 1848, from £23,000 to £52,000—looking to which notable circumstances, one is inclined to feel somewhat incredulous on the score of alleged Irish poverty. Belfast, at all events, possesses one unmistakable evidence of social advancement—a fœtid river and harbour; so loathsome and insalubrious were its waters, that the *Pharos* could not make out the entire Sunday at its handsome quay; and, receiving me on board, dropped down for the night to the open sea adjoining Carrickfergus.

Skirting along the north of Ireland, and then shooting across to the southern points of the Hebrides, I enjoyed my first day at sea. In passing, we took a look of the Giants' Causeway, which all on board pronounced to be a poor affair in comparison to Staffa. At the Rhins of Islay began that systematic visitation of Scottish light-houses which was pursued for the next fourteen days, among the outer and inner islands, and along the coast of the mainland as far as Cape Wrath; from which limit the vessel retraced its course southwards to Oban, leaving the east coast, and Orkney and Shetland Islands, for next season.

With the drawback of generally dull and moist weather, suggestive of an improvement of Scott's well-known lines:

O Caledonia! stern and wild,
Wet-nurse for a poetic child—

and occasionally tossed about in a rather unceremonious way,

life glided on pleasantly in the *Pharos;* there being in it
that nice blending of duty with amusement, good living, and
leisurely converse, which constitutes an enviable mode of
existence—at anyrate, I do not know of anything better in
this world of ours. Five sheriffs, the provost of Inverness,
the senior bailie of Glasgow, the secretary, and myself, made
up the party—a joyous set of mortals, who, with one or two
exceptions, scorned to be sea-sick, in nearly all weathers
played at shovel-board on deck, and quite as regularly made
their appearance at meals as they took to the boat to visit
the several light-houses.

It is customary in these excursions by the *Pharos,* for
one to be chosen 'commodore,' who has the high function of
presiding at table, regulating the routes as well as general
procedure, and of deciding what shall be the daily bill of
fare — in which last capacity he has frequent serious
communings with the cook. Our commodore on this
occasion was the Sheriff of Forfarshire, who happily
tempered power with discretion, kept all in good-humour,
and deservedly received a vote of thanks for his services,
not the least of which consisted in keeping a capital cuisine.
Breakfast at 9 (a Scotch breakfast), lunch at 1, dinner at 6
(full dress), tea at 8, and anything you like at 9 ; all in bed
by a little after 10. Such was the usual routine in the
alimentary department — any modification in the fare,
considering the amount of fresh air and hard work
encountered, being quite out of the question. It added
not a little to the comfort of the party, that the ship
anchored in a quiet bay every evening about dinner-time—
that, in my opinion, contributing materially to digestion—
and did not start on a fresh cruise till 7 next morning,
which allowed a walk of a couple of hours on deck, to

promote a relish for the kipper, the fresh herrings, and the other edibles which at 9 garnished the table of the saloon.

I have never lived for a time on board any vessel so entirely satisfactory as the *Pharos*. With the exact discipline, promptitude, and courtesy observable in warships, it offered the comforts of a well-regulated home—the alimentary arrangements above hinted at ; a library, if you wished to indulge in reading ; and a snug little room on deck, provided with telescopes, charts, and maps, where one might lounge at ease, and be ready to turn out in a moment with field-glass in hand, to scrutinise the wildly picturesque shores of the Hebridean Archipelago.

There was always some little bustle and fun, along with a becoming air of business, on landing. The stoppage and anchoring of the vessel about a quarter of a mile from the shore, the lowering of a boat, into which the party trooped in walking trim, and the serving out of capacious and well-kept sea-cloaks, as a shelter from the spray while darting over the waves, formed the ordinary routine of disembarkation. One thing was never missed—the landing of ' Milo.' All who have sailed in the *Pharos* have made the acquaintance of Milo, a middle-aged, brown water-spaniel, somewhat lazy from not having much to do, but solemn in character, and to all appearance, impressed with the conviction that he is an essential member of the crew. Milo always makes a point of going on shore with the Commissioners, in order to have a ramble about, while they are engaged in their grave official investigations. When the landing is at a precipitous quay, up which you have to climb by a fixed iron ladder, poor Milo is somewhat nonplussed ; but the difficulty is got over by his being placed on the back of one of the sailors, whom he grasps round the neck with his forepaws, carried in which fashion up the steep ladder, he is set down in safety ; and by the same pleasant process of locomotion, he returns to the boat, after enjoying his scamper over the scanty herbage which clothes the rocky promontories.

In these landings, there was considerable uniformity. For the most part, the light-houses are placed on bold head-lands, at a distance varying from a hundred yards to a mile and a half from the landing-place. Each establishment consists not only of a tall stone tower, with its lofty lighting apparatus, but of a cluster of neat dwellings for the keepers, to which, in all cases, there is convenient access from the shore by a road made at the expense of the Commission. The making of these roads forms, in some instances, a heavy item of outlay, but is indispensable for the construction of the works, and afterwards for facilitating the regular and safe transmission of stores. Reaching the spot, and throwing aside walking-sticks and loose upper-coats, the Commissioners mount in the first place by winding stairs and ladders to the summit of the tower ; there they sagaciously examine the bright burnished lamps, lenses, and reflectors—some, perhaps, by dint of repeated investigation, acquiring for the first time an intelligent idea of the difference between the two great modern systems of lighting—the catoptric and dioptric. All, at least, are struck with the singular beauty and ingenuity of the works, and of their great value as regards averting shipwreck and the saving of human life. Noble outposts of humanity and civilisation are these gigantic structures ! Would not any one be proud to take part in their organisation and maintenance !

Large lenses and prisms of different shapes for concentrating and sending forth the rays of light from effulgent oil-lamps, constitute a leading feature in the apparatus. Formerly,

Great Britain could not produce these lenses in perfection, owing to the obstruction to experiment caused by the glass-duties, and our light-houses were therefore supplied with the needful apparatus by France. Now, the works are of home-manufacture, glass, lamps, reflectors, and everything—Chance of Birmingham for lenses, and Milne of Edinburgh for brass and lamp-work, being the main producers; the cost of a fully-equipped apparatus is from £800 to £3000, according to the class and character of the light. The outlay in building a light-house varies, according to dimensions and other circumstances, from £4500 to six times that amount; but sometimes the cost is considerably higher. Something, I learn, in the way of sufficiency, depends on the spirit which happens to influence the Trinity House of England and Board of Trade, which, by statute, exercise a certain control over the operations of the Northern Commission—the Trinity as regards sites and projects, the Board of Trade as regards plans, revenue, and expenditure. It was not always so; and some appear to think that under the new régime the spirit of economy has weighed a little too heavily on the construction and general character of the light-houses lately erected on the dangerous sea-shores of Scotland. A pretty bold attempt was made about sixteen years ago to abolish the Scottish and Irish Boards, and concentrate the entire management in the Trinity House. A recommendation to this effect came, as I think, with a peculiarly bad grace from the Royal Commission employed to look into these affairs; for in drawing a comparison, it had to acknowledge that the 'Scotch light-houses are in the best state of general efficiency, the English next, and the Irish third.' The Northern Commission was accordingly let alone, and continues as effective as ever, under the administration of a vigilant secretary and the body of unpaid officials, who seem to take a surprising degree of interest in its operations. Something of its success is doubtless also due to the Stevensons, a well-known family of engineers, who have done great things for Scottish and colonial light-houses. The late Robert Stevenson, the father, was the eminent constructer of the light-house on the Bell-Rock, and for the Skerryvore we are indebted to his elder son, Alan, recently deceased.

Were I giving a formal history of light-houses, I should specify a number of things which characterise the Scotch establishments, and have led to the foregoing testimony of their marked superiority. I will refer only to what no one can avoid noticing—the respectable appearance of the keepers and their families, the large number of children, the neatness and substantiality of the dwellings, and the air of comfort which universally prevails. One would almost think that a blessing was showered upon the fraternity, in compensation for the exile which all less or more necessarily experience. But it is to be kept in mind that the 'service' is somewhat enviable, and commands a superior class of officers. To the excellent pay of from fifty to seventy guineas a year, are added a uniform, a free furnished house, coal and candle, a garden, and a cow's grass if it can be obtained, books and periodicals—changed about for mutual convenience—medical attendance, and lastly, the visits of a missionary.

When the keepers have to do duty in those light-houses which stand on isolated rocks in the ocean, and must for weeks be absent from their homes, they are, over and above all these various advantages, provided with rations. The Board furnishes the houses of the keepers in every particular, and by means of regular inspectors, preserves the whole in good order. It could not well be otherwise.

Like soldiers on duty, keepers are moved about from place
to place, according to promotion in the service, health, wish
for change, and other causes; and when ordered off to some
new scene, the family has only to carry away its personal
luggage, with perhaps a few fancy articles, such as a
favourite canary in a well-wrapped-up cage, a geranium in
flower, or a stuffed solan goose, prized as a chimney-piece
ornament. Quitting one home, it may be in a wild islet of
Shetland, and reaching another possibly on the more genial
shores of Mull, the wanderers find it a facsimile of that
which they have left — the very eight-day clock, in its
burnished mahogany case, that confronts them as they
enter the new mansion, presenting, as it were, the face of
a well-known friend, and in familiar sounds ticking an
accustomed welcome.

Social economists speculate on plans for making life-
assurance a matter of compulsion. This is done by the
Northern Lights in a way worth describing. From the
annual salary of each man who enters the service, the sum
of £3 is deducted, and laid out in insuring his life. The
insurance is taken in the name of the Commissioners, who,
on the decease of the assured, draw and pay the amount to
his family. According to the age at commencement, the
sum ultimately realised ranges from £100 to £130, and
comes as an acceptable boon to the bereaved widow and
children. The good effected by this arrangement is incalculable. There are likewise retiring allowances for super-
annuated and well-behaved officers.

Comparative seclusion, remoteness from friends, at most
only one or two neighbours with whom to hold rational
converse: Are not these terrible drawbacks on the current
sources of happiness of these light-house keepers? Not at

all. Instances are not unknown of individuals sinking under the quietude and sameness of their mode of life; but these are exceptions. As a general rule, the keepers and their families are a happy set of people, well read as to what is going on in the world, and accustomed to make the best of opportunities for bettering their circumstances. The periodical visits of inspectors, and of the *Pharos* or some other vessel with stores, are events of moment. But the greatest event of all during the year is the arrival of the Commissioners, when the flag is hoisted in their honour, and requests are entered in the note-book of the secretary. Some keepers solace their spare hours with handicrafts. One is a good tinsmith; another amuses himself with a turning-lath and carpenter's bench; and I heard of a third who is noted among the islands as an excellent bootmaker. Setting aside all such useful recreations to fill up the time, let us again remember that these light-house keepers belong to a class of society who value the importance of an assured income, along with the other substantial benefits and social elevation of the service, above mere sentiment. Neither man nor woman whom I talked to complained of loneliness. No; it was not there that the shoe pinched. Revealing, as I thought, a fine trait in the Scottish character, that which only and really detracted from the happiness of the situation, was the difficulty—often the entire impracticability—of getting proper schooling for the children. 'I have not been at church for four years, and scarcely expect to be ever at one again,' said the wife of a keeper. Another whom I spoke to, gets to church twice a year in a boat, the voyage thither being fourteen miles, along a rugged coast full of sunk rocks. However, the desire to do a duty to offspring goes beyond any such consideration. The want of schools is the subject of constant lament ; for without education, how are the children to get on in life. As a make-shift, sometimes an elder girl teaches the younger, or the parents themselves try to take the matter in hand, while the missionary also to a certain extent helps in the business of elementary instruction. I am not without a hope that the Commissioners, with the sanction of the Board of Trade, will fall upon some expedient to insure the education of the numerous children connected with their establishments. A few migratory young schoolmasters making periodical rounds, would go far to remedy the evil.

I inquired if there was much intercourse between the keepers and the widely scattered families of the Gaelic-speaking natives. Very little, was the reply. As a rule, the Board find it necessary to discourage the visits of these poor people to their establishments, on account of personal habits which are adverse to the scrupulous cleanliness insisted on in the dwellings. Those who are acquainted with the miserable condition of the natives of the more remote western islands, will not be surprised at this species of exclusiveness. Wherever placed, the cluster of buildings composing the establishment, with their whitewashed walls, form a kind of oasis in the desert—a bit of civilisation planted and flourishing in the midst of scenes of savage sterility and human degradation.

Mention of these circumstances reminds me that the service has two prizes, to which all keepers with ambitious views properly aspire. These are appointments to the Bell-Rock and Skerryvore, in both of which the keepers reside for weeks in the midst of the ever-surging waves, and only enjoy the society of their families at stated intervals. How do we explain the paradox? Simply enough : higher pay, rations, and chiefly, convenient schooling for children. The Bell-Rock, with a family residence at Arbroath, where schools abound, and employment for children is obtained, was on all hands referred to as the *ne plus ultra* of light-house appointments—a thing sighed for, but not easily obtained, and when quitted, looked back upon as a kind of 'Paradise Lost.'

And now, let us be off for Skerryvore, which some people think, myself for one, is worth travelling a thousand miles to see; but the voyage must be left to another chapter.

CHAPTER II.

OFF for the Skerryvore, but only after the essential preliminary of spending a day at Oban in coaling. Oban, which may be taken to be a kind of metropolis of the Hebrides, is the place set apart for this important particular, and thither the *Pharos* wended its way from Islay and the Sound of Jura. All who are acquainted with the beautiful land-locked bay of Oban, will recollect seeing a strange black hulk composedly anchored near the island of Kerrera, opposite the town, and perhaps they may have wondered why that old and mastless vessel should not be removed and broken up as a useless speck on the scene. That dark mass, however, is not useless, nor is it without a history. It is what remains of the *Enterprise*, a strong-built wooden vessel, which took part in the ill-fated explorations of Sir John Franklin, and which, placed at the disposal of the Commissioners of Northern Light-houses, is employed by them as a repository for coal and miscellaneous stores. Nor is the mass dull and lifeless. It is inhabited by a keeper and his family, who, as things go, find themselves tolerably well off. The hulk, as a western depôt, is often visited for light-house purposes; the children of the keeper are rowed daily ashore to a school at Kerrera; and if the little dog which feels itself to be installed as a guardian of the old battered craft does not often get across the bay to Oban, it can at least reckon on now and then renewing acquaintance with Milo, when the *Pharos* steers alongside, and a broad gangway for wheel-barrows is temporarily established between the two vessels.

There was a day of this gangway intercommunication, during which loads of coal were wheeled by a band of grimy Calibans from the *Enterprise* to the *Pharos*, and the two dogs paid accustomed visits to each other, and in their own way talked over matters of canine interest. The Commissioners, in the meanwhile thrown off work, went on shore at Oban to look after letters and newspapers, and a number of them, by way of filling up the time, set off on a sauntering pedestrian excursion to Dunstaffnage; but I believe they never reached that historical ruin, for all were anxious to return to the ship in good time for the raising of the anchor, it having been determined that as soon as the coaling was over, the ship should make the best of its way for Tobermory in Mull for the night. With all on board, six o'clock saw the *Pharos* once more pursuing its way among the islands.

Early next morning, we were *en route* round the northern extremity of Mull, and with a slight bend southwards to have a glimpse of Staffa, the vessel held on almost straight west to Tyree, a long unpicturesque island, generally low and grassy, with a high rocky extremity presented to the full sweep of the Atlantic. In a small cove near this headland is the harbour of Hynish, at which, while the *Pharos* remains discreetly in the offing, we land to make our inquiries. Milo, of course, is not forgot; on the back of a sailor, who climbs up the ladder at the pier, he is placed amongst us on solid ground, and makes off over the adjoining knolls. The inner part of the small harbour consists of a wet-dock sufficient for the sailing schooner of fifty or sixty tons burden, which is employed in communicating with the Skerryvore light-house, eleven to twelve miles distant.

Hynish, altogether, is but an adjunct of Skerryvore. In the olden time, it may have been a clachan of the Highland type, but now it is nothing more than a settlement of families less or more under the auspices of the Commissioners of Northern Lights; and only after a little scrutiny do we see, on some distant braes, several poor-looking thatched huts spared from inevitable clearance. Like all the establishments for the residence of light-house keepers, that at Hynish is of a most substantial kind; it embraces residences for the families of four keepers, along with dwellings for the men who attend to the small sailing tender, and one or two houses for stores—a community larger than usual, and better off than that of most other places as regards a tolerably near neighbourhood to a church and school, and also medical attendance. Though fertile and mild in climate. Tyree seems to be destitute of trees. The Atlantic blasts would probably prevent their growth, but certainly they offer no check to the vegetables and flowering shrubs with which the walled gardens of the keepers are plentifully stocked.

Behind the settlement, on a conspicuous knoll overlooking the sea on the west, stands a tower of observation for holding intercourse by signal with the lone dwellers on the rock. In the upper floor of the building is placed a large telescope, pointed in the direction of Skerryvore, which some of our party declared they could see like a speck on the dim misty horizon; but this feat was beyond my power of vision. I could see nothing but the great broad ocean, with its long swelling waves, and the sea-birds which wheeled in graceful motion over the coast of the island. Little time was spent in these and other investigations. It was of the utmost importance to reach Skerryvore at low tide, in order to have the best chance of effecting a landing; the weather, though dull, was also still favourable, but both barometer and sympisometer hinted that there should be no undue delay in taking our departure. Off, accordingly, we went, the whole male population respectfully attending on the quay, and watching till the boat had placed us on board the *Pharos*, which instantly steamed away in the required south-western direction.

Of course, all were anxious to catch the first glimpse of Skerryvore, and in spite of cold and damp, took up positions on the bridge of the steamer, in company with Captain Graham, the commander, who directed attention to the point where the tall structure would be seen emerging from the bosom of the deep. And there, sure enough, at length it made its appearance, looming dimly through the dull haze, solitary amidst the world of waters. As the vessel approached this extraordinary work of art, the feeling of those who had not previously seen it was one of intense pleasure and satisfaction. There are sights of such impressive grandeur as cannot be forgotten, and the recollection of which forms one of the charms of existence. Among these I have reckoned the falls of Niagara, the ruins of the Colosseum, and interior of St Peter's, and now am able to add the Skerryvore lighthouse. Its isolation is paralleled at the Bell-Rock and Eddystone, and one or two other places. So far, there is nothing singular. What enchains the mind of the spectator is the remarkable dimensions and matchless beauty of design of the Skerryvore—its elegant curving taper, from the broad and firm base to the summit, and its great height of a hundred and fifty feet to the top of the lantern, which is double the altitude of the Eddystone, and a third higher than the Bell-Rock. There is, however, more to surprise us in the perfection with which the whole is finished, as well as in the depth of thought required in its execution. I believe there is only one loftier light-house in the world. This is the *Tour de Corduan,* situated on a reef of rock at the mouth of the river Garonne, which is a pile rich in architectural details, rising tier above tier to a height of a hundred and ninety-seven feet. Perhaps, after all, the true explanation of the overpowering effect in the Skerryvore is derived from the exceeding simplicity of the structure ; for it seems to combine what mechanical science signifies to be the strongest in material, form, and construction, along with what æsthetics would say is most thoroughly simple and tasteful. But it is only on close examination that we learn fully to appreciate the genius of the constructer.

The *Pharos* having dropped anchor, the party, by means of two boats, were rowed to a narrow inlet or gully in the straggling heap of rocks, which at the low state of the tide shewed a variety of protuberances, on the highest and broadest of which the light-house was planted. Our appearance had brought out the three keepers in their uniforms, and, ready to lend assistance, they helped us to step ashore without difficulty. A pathway of ribbed iron, riveted to the rock, and painted red, enabled us at once to walk forward to the foot of the tower under the doorway, which faces the east. Here, looking around, there was apparently at least an acre of rocks in detached masses visible above the water, with a limited smooth space for walking about on all sides of the building. Dry, and free from marine plants,

the higher part of the ledge was at the time about fifteen
to eighteen feet above the sea-level; and I learned that,
except during heavy storms, the rock adjoining the light-
house, and certain outlying patches, are never entirely
covered. The whole of the ledge, consisting chiefly of a
kind of gneiss ploughed into gullies, in which boulders are
kept ever rolling about, is but a portion of a long stretch of
hard rocks here and there shewing their dangerous presence
by the lashing and fretting of the sea, and on which wrecks
were of frequent occurrence previous to the completion of
the light-house.

As early as 1804, Mr Robert Stevenson paid a visit to
the Skerryvore reef, the terror of homeward-bound mariners,
and again he made a more special investigation of the rock
in 1814, in company with a party of Northern Commissioners
on their annual tour of inspection. On this occasion Walter
Scott accompanied the Commissioners in their sailing yacht,
and, in his own easy and humorous way, has given the
following account of the visit in his diary :

'Having crept upon deck about four in the morning, I
find we are beating to windward off the island of Tyree,
with the determination on the part of Mr Stevenson, that
his constituents should visit a reef of rocks called *Skerry
Vhor*, where he thought it would be essential to have a
light-house. Loud remonstrances on the part of the
Commissioners, who one and all declare they will subscribe
to his opinion, whatever it may be, rather than continue the
infernal buffeting. Quiet perseverance on the part of Mr
S., and great kicking, bouncing, and squabbling upon that
of the yacht, who seems to like the idea of Skerry Vhor as
little as the Commissioners. At length, by dint of exertion,
came in sight of this long ridge of rocks (chiefly under

water), on which the tide breaks in tremendous style. There appear a few low broad rocks at one end of the reef, which is about a mile in length. These are never entirely under water, though the surf dashes over them. To go through all the forms, Hamilton, Duff, and I resolve to land upon these bare rocks in company with Mr Stevenson. Pull through a very heavy swell with great difficulty, and approach a tremendous surf dashing over black pointed rocks. Our rowers, however, get the boat into a quiet creek between two rocks, where we contrive to land well wetted. I saw nothing remarkable in my way excepting several seals, which we might have shot, but, in the doubtful circumstances of the landing, we did not care to bring guns. We took possession of the rock in the name of the Commissioners, and generously bestowed our own great names on its crags and creeks. The rock was carefully measured by Mr S. It will be a most desolate position for a light-house—the Bell-Rock and Eddystone a joke to it, for the nearest land is the wild island of Tyree. So much for the Skerry Vhor.'

Twenty years elapsed after this memorable visit before the Commissioners ordered surveys and plans; and not until 1838 were operations for the establishment of a light-house commenced by Mr Alan Stevenson, to whom is due the glory of planning and perfecting the undertaking. The works were carried on at three places—at Mull, where the stone, a pale reddish granite, was quarried; at Hynish, where all the slabs were shaped and arranged to fit their respective positions; and finally, on the rock. It is scarcely possible to imagine the amount of anxiety and bodily toil endured by the constructer in these varied proceedings. One of the lively episodes in the history of the building was tho destruction, by a storm, of a temporary wooden barrack planted on tho rock for the uso of the operatives. Only by an indomitable degree of courago was the light-house at length completed, after six years of exertion. It says not a little for Mr Stevenson's nicety of calculation, that although tho stones had to bo prepared at Hynish, they did not, on being set in their several courses, vary the sixteenth of an inch, while the building did not exceed half an inch in height over the intended dimension. Nor is it a matter less worthy of note, that throughout the whole of the hazardous undertaking not a single life was lost by accident.

On the 1st of February 1844, the Skerryvore Light for tho first time sent its brilliant rays over the surrounding seas, and human skill may be said to have achieved a new triumph. What was the entire cost of this wonderful work of art, including the establishment and harbour at Hynish? It was £83,000—not a great sum, all things considered. It is a circumstance to bo gratefully borne in mind, that the late Duke of Argylo permitted the stone to be taken free of chargo from his quarries. A very few figures give one a notion of the ponderous character of the light-house. With a foundation sunk fifteen inches in the rock, the base of the edifice is forty-two feet in diameter, and is solid for the first twenty-six feet—to which point the mass of masonry weighs two thousand tons. Above this level, the walls are fully nine and a half feet thick, gradually reduced to two feet, and leaving an interior space of twelve feet in diameter. By an adjustment of weight in reference to the height of the building, tho centre of gravity is kept comparatively low; and with the additional means which aro employed to joint and cement the stones firmly in connection with each other, the whole becomes a species of monolith, which, seemingly, not all the pressure of the sea in its wildest mood is able to disturb.

Let us ascend to the interior. Climbing hand-over-hand up a weather-stained brass ladder attached to the side of the tower, we one by one reach the doorway in the enormously thick wall, and find ourselves in what may be styled the ground-floor of the building. Stone is above, below, and around us, for neither deal flooring nor ceiling enters into the composition. A step-ladder, bent to the interior curve, enables us, by clutching to a brass rail, to reach the next story above; and so on through ten stories we reach the top. In the construction of the stone floor of each story in succession there is much to admire. It consists of an arch, but not of the ordinary kind. From the walls around flat stones are projected and jointed into one central stone, the whole forming a compact mass, level on the top for the floor, and slightly curved on the under side for the ceiling of the story below. These flat stone arches, in which gaps are left for the ladders, are probably of value as regards strengthening the general fabric. The lower stories are used for stores of coal, fresh-water, provisions, and other articles. In one of them were a carpenter's bench and tools. Above are the sitting and sleeping rooms lighted by windows, and fitted up with furnishings of oak. Everything was comfortable and even tasteful; but not more so than was proper for the residence of three men cut off for weeks from intercourse with the outer world. On a window-sole stood a geranium in flower, doubtless an importation from the gardens at Hynish. The highest floor of all, as in the other lighthouses under the Commissioners, is provided with a table and chair, with writing materials, along with a book for inscribing the names of visitors; we also find a shelf with books and periodicals to wile away the hours during watch, and a framed list of the exact time for lighting up and extinguishing the lamp daily over the whole year. On this last-mentioned particular, the system prevalent at the Scottish light-houses deserves special notice. Instead of lighting up at sunset, and extinguishing at sunrise, as is the practice, I believe, in England and elsewhere, the plan consists in making allowance for the long periods of twilight in northern latitudes, more especially in the summer months, when, although the sun is below the horizon, there is in reality good daylight. Tables are calculated accordingly, from actual observation in the different localities. By adopting this plan of lighting, the Northern Commissioners effect a saving in oil of not less than £1600 a year.

Here, as elsewhere, the arrangement for the keepers is to watch four hours alternately, and on no account whatever is one to leave until another takes his place. The watcher can readily communicate with the apartment of the sleeper who is to succeed, by blowing through a small tube in the wall, which produces the sound of a bell. Sitting on duty in this upper apartment, the keeper has overhead the great blaze of light effected by the central lamp, which, according to the dioptric method, shines through annular lenses; beside him, in the centre of the apartment, is the mechanism, in the form of clock-work, by which the frame of lenses revolves, and causes an alteration of darkness and a bright blaze of light every minute. By a narrow ladder we ascended to the iron gangway around the apparatus of lenses, and had the process of lighting explained. The light, when at the moment of greatest brilliance, can be seen at a distance of eighteen miles on the sea-level. Its appearance is a warning to avoid the foul ground in the neighbourhood, of which

Admiralty charts give the fullest intimation. From the floor occupied by the man on duty, there is an outlet by a door to the exterior balcony, on which is placed a bell to be struck as a fog-signal. We examined the bell. By an adaptation of the clock-work, it can be made to sound at regular intervals, but it is doubtful if these signals of danger can be heard at any great distance. My own experience of a fog, on one occasion in crossing the Channel to Calais, where a bell was kept tolling, leads to the supposition that bells can be heard but a short way off during a thick palpable fog, and are of little practical avail.

As the weather had partially cleared, we had a pretty extensive view over the waste of waters from the balcony. The only visible land was that of Tyree at Hynish, with its signal-tower. I was interested in knowing the method of intercourse by signals. Every morning between nine and ten o'clock, a ball is to be hoisted at the light-house to signify that all is well at the Skerryvore. Should this signal fail to be given, a ball is raised at Hynish to inquire if anything is wrong. Should no reply be made by the hoisting of the ball, the schooner, hurried from its wet-dock, is put to sea, and steers for the light-house. Three men are constantly on the rock, where each remains six weeks, and then has a fortnight on shore; the shift, which is made at low water of spring tides, occurs for each in succession, and is managed without difficulty by means of the fourth or spare keeper at Hynish, who takes his regular turn of duty. According to these arrangements, the keepers of the Skerryvore are about nine months on the rock, and about three months with their families every year. But this regularity may be deranged by the weather. One of the keepers told me that last winter he was confined to the rock for thirteen weeks, in consequence of the troubled state of the sea preventing personal communication with the shore. I inquired how high the waves washed up the sides of the tower during the most severe storms, and was told that they sometimes rose as high as the first window, or about sixty feet above the level of the rocks; yet, that even in these frightful tumults of winds and waves, the building never shook, and no apprehension of danger was entertained.

When the weather is fine, the keepers are not by any means confined to the building. They may straggle about among the gullies, enjoy the fresh air, and amuse themselves by angling for the smaller kinds of white-fish; any catch of this sort imparting a little relish to the monotony of the daily fare. The visits of seals, which are occasionally seen frisking in the surf, also furnish some amusement, and one can fancy that, to a student of natural history, life at the Skerryvore might furnish some useful memoranda. The keepers, as previously mentioned, do not complain of solitude; the obligations of professional duty, and the periodical return to their families at Hynish, where in fine weather they occupy themselves with their gardens, help materially to banish the sense of loneliness. Besides, as we observed from the visitors' book, yachting-parties sometimes land on the rock, and ascend to the top of the light-house, perhaps leaving behind them the acceptable gift of a few newspapers, to shew what is going on in the outer world. The Commissioners do not object to the visits of respectable parties to this or any other light-house under their charge, for they believe that such visits, when properly conducted, may be in various ways beneficial.

We spent an hour on the rock; more time could have been agreeably occupied, but the Commissioners of Northern

Lights act as men of business, and have little to charge themselves with in the way of procrastination. There was other work to be done before night. We had to reach a bay behind Barra Head, the bold southern promontory of that long series of islands and rocks which stretch northwards and terminate in the Butt of Lewis. The *Pharos*, with all safely on board, is therefore to be supposed once more pushing onward in its course. My last look of this giant of the ocean embraced the three keepers standing at gaze on an elevated peak of the rock, but the rising mist and increasing distance soon shut them from our view; and Skerryvore remained only as one of the pleasing remembrances of my excursion.

CHAPTER III.

LEAVING Skerryvore wrapped in the rising mists, the *Pharos* went steadily on its way in a north-westerly direction for Barra-Head, on the small island of Bernera, which may, from its great height, in clear weather be seen from a considerable distance. In present circumstances, it did not become visible till we were within ten miles of its light-house, situated on the summit of the precipitous crag. The value of the Barra-Head light can be easily conjectured, for shipwreck on the cliffs beneath would be instantaneous destruction.

With the headland on our left, the *Pharos* rounded into a sheltered bay, where it dropped anchor for the night. Properly speaking, the bay was a channel between two islands, Bernera and Mingalay; but intersected as it is with huge rocks near its western extremity, it is impracticable for navigation. Both islands and some others are often collectively styled Barra, from the larger of the group, and

hence the terminating point of the most southerly receives
the designation Barra-Head. Our business was exclusively
with this famed promontory, and to reach it, there was
before us a pretty long walk up-hill. Overnight, it was
resolved in full conclave that the walk should be performed
next morning before breakfast, as there was a long day's
work afterwards; but as this was deemed to be exacting in
the way of duty—in fact, against all rule, and not to be
construed into a precedent—cups of coffee were to be
considerately served all round before starting. So fortified,
the Commissioners were next morning rowed ashore about
seven o'clock, and made their landing on Bernera at an inlet
in a long stretch of dry rocks, dotted over with quantities of
fish in the process of being cured for export. With Milo as
a sort of scout in advance, all sturdily betook themselves to
the ascent. The road slanted upward across the open
hillside, which was devoted chiefly to the pasturage of a
few cattle and sheep. Here and there were small patches
of barley and oats, enclosed with fences of turf; but so
meagre were the crops, and so plentifully interspersed with
tall dock-weeds, that there was promise of but an insignificant
harvest. The tenants of these crofts, as far as I could see,
were the dwellers in two or three thatched huts by the
wayside. Nearly half-way up, I called attention to a
phenomenon in these parts—a low building which appeared
to be a mill of some kind, with a wheel at one end, movable
by a rill of water from the grounds above.

After a stiff pull, we at length reach the light-house
establishment, which, with its environing walls and gates
has somewhat the aspect of a fortification. The whole of
the buildings are of a beautiful white granite, quarried in
the island. As in similar cases, the transition from the

rough state of things outside the establishment to the
orderly arrangements within, was an abrupt step from
medieval to modern times. An interior paved court is
environed by the houses of three keepers ; and passing them,
we reach the tower for the light, with its winding stair,
which all immediately ascend, preceded by one of the
keepers. What an outlook from the upper story down to
the sea, which surges seven hundred feet below ; and what
myriads of sea-birds screaming and fluttering on ledges of
this tremendous precipice ! I have seen it stated that these
cliffs excel in grandeur anything of the kind in the Hebrides.
and can scarcely doubt that such is the case. On a
projecting point immediately in front of the light-house, are
the ruins of an old castle or keep, once the stronghold of
some Hebridean chief. As usual, before departure, we visited
the several houses of the keepers, and entered into a little
friendly conversation on matters of domestic interest. In
one of the dwellings, some information was picked up
respecting the water-mill which had excited our curiosity.
The mill is entirely the handiwork of an ingenious assistant
light-house keeper (a Fife man), who diverted his leisure
hours in its construction. He erected the building, covered
it with a tarpauling roof, and fabricated the whole of the
grinding apparatus. The most difficult part of the undertaking was accomplished by adapting an old cart-wheel.
The idea of erecting a mill was suggested by the absence
from the island of all means for grinding except by a primitive species of hand-querns. It turned out to be a grand
conception this mill. Glad of the opportunity of so easily
transforming their corn into meal, the crofters besought the
privilege of using it, which was of course allowed ; and as
money happens to be a rare article in Bernera, the multure

was arranged on the convenient footing of giving a lamb for a grist, be the quantity much or little.

Returning leisurely before the others, I had time to inspect the interior of the mill, which I found to be about eight feet square, and lighted only by the low doorway; adjoining is a kiln, equally diminutive, made, as I was told, from a piece of old sheet-iron, and indispensable for drying the parcels of grain which are taken to this modest establishment to be ground. I afterwards took the liberty of visiting two thatched dwellings of the well-known Western Island type—poor lowly biggings, with no attempt at either neatness or cleanliness in their miserable surroundings. Let me just say a word or two about dwellings of this sort. A leading feature consists in a twisted orifice in the roof, to let out the smoke as it ascends from the peat-fire in the middle of the clay-floor—the said twist being adjusted so as to keep the rain from falling directly down over the fire, which would not be pleasant. Two things are obviously disliked in this quarter of the world—chimneys and windows. The great enemy is cold, which would be radiated from windows of ordinary size; and with a chimney constructed in the wall of the house, the family could not sit round the fire. If the smoke does not shoot immediately upwards, so much the better; hovering overhead, it keeps the dwelling warm, and shrouds all in that fine indistinctness which affords play to the imagination. It is, however, not altogether for such reasons that the inmates of these cabins dislike slated roofs. Thatch offers a particular advantage. When sufficiently rotted with damp, and well saturated with soot, it forms an esteemed manure, and is carried away in backloads to the arable plots in the vicinity; wherefore each house may be said to be a dungheap in preparation, such as Mr Mechi, I venture to think, has not yet introduced into his marvellously economical systems of husbandry.

I had learned, from various knowing hints and looks of a Commissioner, that it was not advisable to enter any of the dwellings organised on these admired principles, but had no reason to regret having disregarded the well-meant intimations. In the first hut I entered there was an old woman barefooted, who could speak only a few words of English, but seemed anxious to be hospitable, and set a chair for me beside the peat-fire. Though small, smoky, and dingy, the cottage contained a loom in one corner, in which was a web of dark woollen cloth, which the woman made me understand was for the clothing of the family. In the other hut there were an old woman carding wool, and her daughter neatly dressed in tartan, who spoke English tolerably. Here, also, was a loom, at which the daughter wove the family woollen clothing ; a circumstance shewing no little thrift and ingenuity. The husband and sons connected with these families, as I understood, occupy their time partly as fishermen, and at certain seasons take cargoes of cured fish in their open boats to Portrush, on the northern coast of Ireland, or sell them to Glasgow traders. What with the hill-pastures, the arable patches, and the sea, there was apparently no deficiency as regards means of living; and if existence in these smoky dens did not seem altogether enviable, I was constrained to remember that I had not long since visited dwellings in the closes of the Old Town of Edinburgh quite as dingy, and infinitely more revolting. In the last of my civic explorations, I had seen a dwelling in Toddrick's Wynd consisting of a single dungeon-looking apartment, without a window, in which ten persons of different sexes habitually lived, but one of whom, by a not unusual casualty, happened at the time to be in prison. After spectacles of this nature so near home, and which the world takes very complacently, it would be ridiculous to bear hard on the domiciliary condition of these Bernera crofters.

All on board by half-past nine, and the *Pharos* once more under steam, taking its course along the east side of Barra, South Uist, Benbecula, North Uist, and a number of intermediate islands, and stopping for a short time midway to admit of a visit to the light-house of Ushenish. The programme indicated that the Commissioners were to visit the Monach light, on the western side of the islands, which the vessel was to reach through a navigable channel; but the weather proved too stormy for us to face the Atlantic, or to attempt a landing in that direction; the *Pharos* therefore pursued its way to Lochmaddy, a well-sheltered bay in North Uist, where it was to remain for the night. Cold and gusty as the day happened to be, most of the party kept the deck, and occasionally mounted to the bridge, with field-glass in hand, to catch glimpses of the rugged coast, which appeared a strange combination of rocks, low unpicturesque hills, and inlets of the sea. Some amusement was derived from the notion that part of this ungenial domain was the ancient patrimony of the M'Neills of Barra, who at one time assumed the airs of independent sovereignty, and, according to Carstairs's state-papers, had sent a magniloquent letter offering aid to the Earl of Argyle. The best of the traditions regarding these self-sufficient old chieftains, is that of the daily proclamation, in Gaelic, from the top of their castle of Chisamil: 'Hear, O ye people! and listen, O ye nations! The great M'Neill of Barra having finished his dinner, all the princes of the earth are at liberty to dine!' Seen from the east side, Barra and the other islands we were passing did not seem qualified to furnish a dinner; but that there might be no mistake on this point, Captain Graham let us know that the belt of fertility stretched along the west side, and that there the sea-shores were remarkably rich in cockles and other varieties of mollusks; from which I would infer, that with a reasonable degree of diligence on the part of his caterer, the great M'Neill never wanted for a good dish of lobster at his famous entertainments. Be this as it might, there can be no doubt that the seas hereabouts are not a half nor a tenth part fished. I would almost go the length of saying, that members of the cod, ling, and sethe tribes jostle each other in their anxiety to be caught and eaten; when baited lines were thrown overboard while the vessel was at rest, hauls were rapidly made, of which cooked specimens duly made their appearance in the saloon.

The reverend minister of Barra, writing in 1840, tells us that the great majority of the inhabitants were Roman Catholics; and the same thing is said by the incumbent of South Uist respecting his parishioners; but as we go northwards, Protestantism in the Presbyterian form gains as remarkable a predominance. This diversified religious condition of the Western Isles is exceedingly curious. It is historical. From the possessions of certain chiefs, the Reformation was somehow excluded, and three centuries have failed to make any great change in this respect. Not only in language and style of living, but in religious sentiment, people are here seen much as their predecessors were immediately after Columba, in the sixth century, propagated a knowledge of Christianity in these insular Caledonian regions. Any one having a fancy to see what Scotland generally was like a thousand years ago, may go to Barra—that is to say, if he can manage to get to it, which may be no easy matter. The extreme difficulty of visiting this and other outlying islands must have acted detrimentally on their interests. The mere trouble of getting from island to island across narrow sounds is annoying. Through these channels, the tides run with a violence that no ordinary boat can withstand. At low water, a number of the channels are dry, and at such times they become excellent fords for traffic by carts or otherwise, on which account the exact state of the tides is a matter of vital solicitude to the islanders. To wish a wayfarer 'a pleasant ford' is something more than an idle compliment; for if he misses the nick of time to make his passage, a delay of twelve hours in his journey may chance to be his fate. From perhaps this as well as other causes, post-letters take a desperately long time to make their way through this part of the Western Isles, which, but for the touching of one of Hutcheson's Glasgow steamers once a fortnight at Lochmaddy, would still be deprived of nearly all regular means of communication for goods or passengers.

Lochmaddy was to us a desirable haven, for the weather was hourly growing worse, and all were glad when, within the shelter of the bay, two anchors were dropped, to keep all secure till morning. As could be seen through our glasses, there was no town on the shore; only two or three buildings with slated roofs, one of which was said to be the house of the sheriff-substitute; and this resident magistrate, by way of compliment to the Commissioners, politely hoisted his flag as we next morning departed on our assigned course. This day, Saturday, August 4th, weather continues cold and boisterous; few keep the deck, but all, with two exceptions, of whom I am one, are able to go off in the boat to visit two light-houses. The last of these establishments was on the point of land on turning into Stornoway Bay; and getting this piece of duty over, the vessel was at its anchorage just in time to allow of dinner being served with some degree of comfort.

Stornoway, I should say, is a good place for finishing off a week's cruise. It offers a fair choice of churches for Sunday, and in this respect it was fully taken advantage of by our party, as well as by the ship's officers, for the weather had temporarily calmed, the sun shone, and a walk on dry land was a luxury which no one could despise. Built in a semicircle at the inner end of the bay, Stornoway appeared to be a rudimentary kind of Oban; but in place of the high, picturesque background of that pretty West Highland town, we have, as the only object of interest, the castellated mansion of Sir James Matheson, the munificent improver of the Lewis, and of this seaport in particular. Between ten and eleven o'clock, two boatfuls are set on shore at the slip of quay, and all make off for their respective places of public worship. About an hour too early for the one I am bound for, there is time to look about, and see what is going on. Shops all decently shut, and men and women pouring in streams from different quarters towards a central point, to which they are lugging along chairs or stools as seats for an open-air preaching. Dropping into the concourse, I am led to a grassy field with environing walls, having a wide gateway, at each side of which stands a man gathering halfpence in a dinner-plate. A tent is placed at one end of the area for the preacher, and stretching half-way across the enclosure is a table decorously covered for dispensing the communion. The scene, with its great crowd of worshippers, was solemn, and more than usually interesting; but as the service was in Gaelic, I listened without edification, and did not remain longer than was necessary to satisfy a reasonable curiosity.

I saw little more of Stornoway. On returning to the ship after attending church, the effects of the last two or three chilly days, and perhaps some over-fatigue, rendered it advisable that I should betake myself to bed; and greatly to my regret, I was robbed of the opportunity of enjoying the kindly proffered hospitality of Stornoway Castle, and learning something coherent of those physical and social improvements on the Lewis which have far and wide spread the renown of Sir James Matheson. Well pleased I should have been had my brother Commissioners seen the desirableness of staying at Stornoway over Monday; but it was resolved otherwise, and in the face of a gale which rendered a visit to the light-house at the Butt of Lewis altogether impracticable, the *Pharos*, as if determined to get into a mischief, was again on its travels. To all appearance, the storm had been reserving itself till we got fairly outside, and then what an uproar of winds and waves! Nothing for it but to give up, *instanter*, the northerly direction to the Butt, and fly eastward across the Minch to some quiet bay on the coast of Sutherlandshire. Bad as things were, no one had the least fear of the *Pharos* coming to any disaster, for, strongly built, and broad in the beam, it swept on its course in gallant style, and about mid-day took us all safely into Lochinchard. Having properly punished our audacity, the weather, as if by magic, suddenly changed to the brightness of a tranquil summer day. Party go on shore to fish in a small river in the neighbourhood—two of the sheriffs, great in the angling art, bring back a grilse and salmon-trout—I am again on my legs, and able to assist at dinner, at which there is not a little merriment over the day's adventures. A degree of novelty at table was the presence of a country doctor, whom the angling party had discovered on his journey to some distant scene of professional duty. This young gentleman let us have an idea of what was a Highland doctor's course of life. His range of practice was over sixty miles in different directions. Sometimes he was on horseback two days at a time, bivouacking at farmhouses and shielings by the way; and no sooner did he get home after these excursions, than he had to be off somewhere else. The narration of these circumstances reminded me of a saying of Mungo Park, that his toil and distraction during his first travels in Africa were nothing in comparison to what he endured in the ill-requited practice of a Scottish country surgeon.

A light-house keeper with his family from Pladda had made his way as far as Stornoway, *en route* for Cape Wrath. Received on board the *Pharos*, he was landed with his wife, bairns, and boxes at Lochinchard, whence he was directed to proceed by a cart to the place of his destination. To the general surprise, the whole boat-load were brought back to the vessel. The people at the inn had a cart, which was at the man's service; but the only two horses in the establishment were lame, which was as bad as having no cart at all. Family once more stowed away somewhere on board till next morning, when, if storm do not reappear, they are to be taken on to Cape Wrath. Fortunately, next morning the weather had taken itself up; by an early start, we were off the Cape by seven o'clock, and saw before us that grand sweep of rugged precipices which constitute the north-western extremity of the island of Great Britain. Here the knocked-about light-house keeper was landed, and installed at his post by the Commissioners; they bringing back with them a keeper who had been promoted to Skerryvore. So adroit are the arrangements of the service, that the ingoing of one family and the outgoing of another scarcely occupied an hour. An object of special care on the part of this new family, whom we were taking with us as far as Portree, was a hen with a brood of infantile chickens under her wings, the whole very nicely accommodated in a basket, and which, unconscious of the change, are now doubtless picking their way comfortably about at Hynish.

At Cape Wrath, the captain had his suspicions as to the weather. Things did not look well in the north-west; and when returning southward along the coast of the mainland, the storm resumed its fury. Driving onward before the misty blast, any attempt to land on the island of Rona, to inspect the light-house, was deemed hopeless; and the vessel did not stop in its course till it arrived in the evening at Portree in Skye. The bay of Portree, land-locked and sheltered like a placid basin from the outer storms, was to us a pleasant haven of rest; and further, it enabled us to procure some much-needed public intelligence. From the *Clansman*, one of Hutcheson's steamers, without which the social condition of the Western Isles would still cut a sorry figure, we procured Glasgow morning newspapers of the day of our arrival; after perusing which, we sauntered about for an hour on shore, admiring the beauty of the scene from a prominent woody knoll overlooking the town and bay; and while admiring, remembered that the spot had been visited by James V. of Scotland on his celebrated hydrographic expedition round the coast in 1540.

Next day, resuming our route, the voyage of the *Pharos* was greatly more pleasant through the sinuous channel of Kyleakin —a name ever commemorative of Haco of Norway and his maritime exploits; after visiting the light-house at that picturesque strait, also one at Isle Oronsay, and another on the bold promontory of Ardnamurchan, night saw us back to our old anchorage at Tobermory.

I have little more to tell. Had I set myself to write a book, instead of a few off-hand sketches, how easy—and perhaps how agreeable—it would have been to scatter in a variety of statistical details and conversational anecdotes, along with a seasoning of territorial and family history! What could not one say about that marvellous change of ownership in the Highlands—the transference of vast estates from the Mackenzies, Mackays, Macleans, Macdonnels, and a dozen other Macs, with a few Campbells to boot, all high chiefs in their day, to the Mathesons, Baillies, Ellises, Bairds, Dalgleishes, Ramsays, and so on. And what strange tales about rise of rental in the hands of these men of the modern world! How could we also expatiate on the character of the natives on mainland and island; describing with what patience and good-behaviour these poor people have suffered vicissitudes such as few are well acquainted with. And then, how the pen would dilate on the wisdom of their unmurmuring submission to lawful authority—how by such propriety of demeanour they have in reality conquered and absorbed the Sassenach, allured him to abide in their wild glens, made him a grateful landlord, furnished him with a following of gillies, put him in kilts, and actually taught him to be fond of the bagpipe, and to dance the Highland fling!

All that and much more must be left to some one with a little more time on his hand than I just now happen to have at my disposal. After visiting the light-house on the point of land near Tobermory, Thursday the last day of our trip was devoted to the light-houses of Lismore and Coran Ferry on Linnhe Loch, familiar to all tourists to Glencoe and the Caledonian Canal. At Oban, on the morning of Friday the 10th of August, proceedings were brought to a close; and respectfully conveyed by boats to the quay, the Northern Commissioners dispersed on their respective routes homeward. So ends MY FIRST HOLIDAY.

MY SECOND HOLIDAY.

A WILD and seemingly persistent gale from the north-east, drenching showers of rain, with thick mists shrouding the sky and hovering over the turbulent waters of the Firth of Forth. Such was the unaccountable state of the weather at Edinburgh on the morning of Monday the 22d of July 1867—a season when one might reasonably have reckoned on something like summer and its accustomed sunshine. It was at least under an expectation of this sort that the Commissioners of Northern Light-houses had arranged to start with the *Pharos* steamer, on their annual voyage of inspection. Fixed securely to the pier at Granton, there lay the vessel, primed with coal, and equipped with all manner of stores for bodily comfort, ready for sea at a moment's notice, or, as the captain said—'Only about twenty minutes wanted to get up the steam, sir, and be off.' But to think of being off in the face of that resolute north-easter, and its dense fogs and drizzle, was sheer nonsense. The voyage was to be along the eastern coast of Scotland to Orkney and Shetland : light-houses perched on craggy eminences, at which landing can be effected only in fine weather, were to be visited here and there along the whole route. Obviously, the thing was out of the question.

At nine o'clock, when I ought to think of moving, I look out of windows back and front, to see if there be any prospect of clearing. None whatever. The sky all round is inexorably dull—not the faintest break—rain remorseless in its pelting fury. At a loss what to do or think, I am relieved by the entrance of a visitor.

'I have just called to ask your Lordship what is to be done,' said the Secretary of the Commissioners, with a face of extreme perplexity. 'The weather seems hopeless; but, on the other hand, if we don't start, the programme for the different voyages will be inconveniently deranged.'

In this latter view of the case lay the real difficulty. On former occasions, the *Pharos* had taken the east coast one year, and the west coast another; but now it was considered preferable to inspect the whole light-houses (weather permitting) every year. This was to be effected by three voyages in succession, each with its distinct party of Commissioners; if the first party, therefore, did not keep the prescribed time, there would necessarily be a general and awkward derangement.

'What has usually been done in circumstances of this kind?' I inquired, for I find it a safe thing in official life to go a good deal by precedent.

'Such a thing as detention by weather never occurred before in all my experience,' said the Secretary with a marked degree of astonishment.

'Well, then, you will at once send for Captain Graham to consult with us at eleven o'clock at your office—down with a cab to Granton for him immediately.'

Scene—Office of Northern Lights in George Street, at

eleven, Captain, Secretary, and two Commissioners—namely, the Sheriff of Caithness and myself—are in grave consultation, rain still driving furiously outside; hardly anybody to be seen moving about; my horses dripping in meek patience, and perhaps meditating on the comforts of the stable from which they have been ruthlessly dragged that terrible morning.

The resolution come to is, that the *Pharos* must remain *in situ* till to-morrow morning after breakfast; but that, on the chance of the weather moderating, the Commissioners, and the friends who are to accompany them, must be on board to-day in time for dinner. A wise determination, worthy to be followed in all similar circumstances. It was not the less judicious, that not even next day, nor next again, did the wind, rain, and fog abate, during which protracted period, what could the luckless Commissioners do but make themselves as comfortable as possible? They were enjoying life at sea, with the peculiar advantage of lying tranquilly in harbour, and receiving the visits of acquaintances.

On Thursday, the weather shews symptoms of mending. The captain, who for three days has been examining the aneroid barometer in the chart-room every ten minutes, reports that there is at last a slight movement in the right direction; and further, that the commander of the *St Magnus*, which has just arrived from Lerwick, communicates the cheering intelligence that he left Bressay Sound basking in sunshine. Hopes of a speedy departure rise high on board the *Pharos*. Captain and mate think we may venture to cast off at four o'clock in the afternoon, when we shall be helped by the tide. As commodore— for to this maritime honour I had been promoted by the Commissioners—I sanction the order for departure accordingly. Stores, a little impaired by recent proceedings, are reinvigorated by fresh importations. Things are decidedly looking up.

The delay, which had been manfully borne by the Commissioners for three mortal days by dint of such services as could be rendered by the cook and steward's departments, had proved to me a special benefit. I was able to do some public business in the interval which I could not complacently have left undone. Up till the last available minute, I was occupied with the ceremonial of delivering prizes at the High School; and rushing away from this academic demonstration, I was just in time to reach the *Pharos*, when the loud rustling of the spare steam plainly indicated that everything was at length ready for departure down the still troubled Firth.

A few notes, written from memory, will explain what followed.

Thursday, July 25.—*Pharos* is let loose at 4.15 P.M. A lady, wife of one of the Commissioners, having bidden goodbye, waits to see the vessel leave the harbour. Interested in Shetland, her last words, patriotically cried to us from the pier, are: 'Mind to go to Scalloway; try to see Foulah.' 'Ay, ay'—handkerchiefs are mutually waved, till increasing distance and the dull creeping haze obscure the shore, from which we are rapidly separated. It is cold; some turn in. I call the Commissioners together and resolve on line of route. All agree that, in consequence of the loss of time, as well as the state of the weather, it is advisable to abandon that part of the programme which refers to the visiting of St Abb's Head and other light-houses along the coast of the mainland. There is nothing now for it but to drive right on to Shetland.

This resolution was contrary to ordinary practice, for the rule, as formerly stated by me, is, to anchor every evening in a quiet bay, previous to sitting down to dinner. Nor is this a very unreasonable arrangement. The Commissioners are not paid officials, and considering their frequent attendance at meetings, as well as the other work they perform, it would be rather too bad to expect that, in their annual inspections, they should make the unbecoming sacrifice of sailing night and day. I entirely coincide in the propriety of not beginning to make any noise on board before six, and not starting before seven o'clock in the morning—of 'doing' not more than two or three light-houses in the day (which is quite enough, as some of them are more than two hundred steps high, with steep ladders at top); and of casting anchor in a sheltered haven for the night. These primary rules are to be invaded only on some particular emergency, as on the present occasion.

On and on, the vessel drove in its course, passing in the dusk the Bell Rock light-house, which blazed forth in solitary grandeur over the waste of tumbling waters. The Bell Rock light-house was one which we were to visit, according to the programme, but that was now impossible. The rock can only be visited deliberately at low water, when a large part of it is exposed, and boats are able to sail into a kind of creek, whence we scramble to the base of the tower. In the course of a visit to it, in September 1866, on the occasion of the *Pharos* delivering oil and other stores, I had an opportunity of inspecting this interesting triumph of art, the work of the late Robert Stevenson. The erection of the Bell Rock light-house occupied from 1807 till February 1811, and cost £60,000. Its height is one hundred feet; at full tide, the sea reaches five or six feet above the base,

but during storms the waves dash much higher, and the
spray is sometimes carried by the force of gales as high as
the lantern. The light is a revolving one, red and white.
In one of the small apartments occupied by the keepers, is
a remarkably fine bust of the constructer, who died 1850.
In 1814, the Bell Rock was visited by Sir Walter Scott,
who, on inscribing his name in the album of the tower,
wrote the following often-quoted lines :

> Far on the bosom of the deep,
> O'er these wild shelves my watch I keep ;
> A ruddy gem of changeful light,
> Bound on the dusky brow of night :
> The seaman bids my lustre hail,
> And scorns to strike his timorous sail.

In Mr Stevenson's account of his operations at the Bell
Rock, forming a portly and highly-illustrated volume, it is
mentioned, that with a view to benefiting the keepers of the
light-house, a quantity of mussels of a large variety were
removed from the sea-shore at Arbroath, and planted on the
shelving rocks around the tower. This well-meant attempt
at colonisation failed in its object in consequence of the
marauding proceedings of the small buckies—*Buccinum
lapillis.* These animals, which seemed to lead an innocent
sort of life among the crevices of the rocks, by means of a
proboscis more powerful than any gimlet, bored holes in the
unfortunate mussels and sucked them clean out. With this
hint, that mussel-culture has no chance of success where
buckies possess the field, I may bid good-bye to the Bell
Rock light-house as it blazed on 'the dusky brow of night,'
and attend to the matter immediately in hand.

Friday, July 26.—Gale and mist still continue. The
Pharos, which is a capital sea-boat, broad in the beam, and

can do ten miles an hour to a nicety, goes pushing busily on all day out of sight of land. There is an ugly twisting sea. which causes a kind of mixture of rolling and pitching, not easy to put up with. One or two have a touch of the *mal de mer*. It is so cold, that there is little walking on deck. Along with the tried hands, I won't give in, and, to set a good example, make a point of attending all the meals, of which I introduce a new one—coffee to be on the table every morning at seven, for those who get up early, and who wish to take something before the *grand déjeúne* at nine. This novelty highly approved of.

Towards the close of day it is announced that Fair Isle is in view. We forthwith run upon deck wrapped in cloaks. and there to be sure is seen the first of the Shetland group. lying at the distance of several miles. It is a high rocky island, but we do not distinguish more than its outlines. and we have no time to pay it a visit. This I regret, for Fair Isle possesses some historical, if not social, interest. It was in this remote island that one of the ships of the Spanish Armada, in which was the Duke of Medina Sidonia, was wrecked, in the attempt to escape northwards in 1588 ; and from the Spaniards who were thus thrown on the hospitality of the natives was derived that taste for dyeing knitted woollen articles for which the island has ever since been noted. The colours employed are blue, yellow, and red in different tints, such as are seen in the woollen productions of Cadiz, and figures of the Maltese cross are usually blended in the patterns. Fair Isle was lately sold to a new proprietor ; but such, I am told, is the poverty of the inhabitants, that the purchase is probably not of a very enviable kind.

Somewhat later, we see Foula, a huge mass, situated far

in the distance on the western horizon, under the golden light of the setting sun ; and when darkness approaches, we have before us the loftily-perched light-house of Sumburgh Head.   The light is one we are to visit ; but meanwhile it must be passed.   On the outlook, the keepers are aware of our proximity, and hoist their flag, which is faintly observed fluttering in the night-breeze at the summit of the cliff.   Some miles further we have yet to go, skirting the eastern side of the mainland of Shetland.   Not until about ten o'clock does the *Pharos* round to the left into Leven-wick Bay, and drop anchor, after a run of thirty hours from Granton.   All at once, the grinding noise of the engine ceases.   We are in profound quiet.   The relief to the sensations is immense.

Saturday, July 27.—Up steam, and off at seven, and again on our travels northwards.   The first object of interest that comes in our way is Noss Head, a bold and lofty precipice, upwards of six hundred feet high, and against the base of which the sea eternally rages, scooping out the lower and more friable strata, so as to cause great caverns and strangely shaped stacks.   One of the largest of the detached masses was formerly reached by adventurous fowlers being drawn in a basket along a cord at the top of the cliff ; but the 'cradle of Noss,' as this aërial machine was termed, has been given up, not only on account of its danger, but as being too attractive to crowds of strangers who were troublesome to the farmer of the adjoining lands. We had a capital sight of this magnificent headland from the deck of the *Pharos*, which approaching to within a distance of a hundred yards, paused in its course for about a quarter of an hour, to enable us to realise the imposing grandeur of the scene.   The reddish-coloured strata formed long and narrow shelves, rising tier above tier, on which sat myriads of white sea-fowl in regular rows, looking out placidly on the ocean. To discompose their deliberations, the two brass guns belonging to the vessel were loaded with powder, and fired cliffward one after the other. The astonishment must have been bewildering to these dwellers

Cradle of Noss.

of the rocks, for immediately they filled the air so thickly as to have the appearance of a shower of snow. Off the whole winged their flight tumultuously eastward, and, for anything I know, they did not recover their equanimity, or stop in their headlong course, till they reached the coast of Norway.

It may be supposed that the weather had somewhat cleared up to permit of this manœuvre; certainly, the drizzle and fog had vanished, and the wind was lulled, but the sea continued to roll on in angry surges, and it was not a little mortifying to have to pass the light-house at Whalsay Skerries about noon without being able to effect a landing.

Again the Commissioners meet to consult as to proceedings, and it is thought expedient to seek a harbourage in Balta Sound, in North Unst, cast anchor, and remain over Sunday. The Sound, I was told, is a land-locked bay, and as tranquil as a pond; which information proved correct. The vessel steamed quietly to its moorings. All around was a bleak country, rising to hills of moderate height; no trees, and few enclosures of any kind, with huts of the humble thatched type, such as one sees in Skye and other western islands. We recognise two houses, built in proper style, and slated. One of them, Buness, the residence of Mr Edmonston, the udaller or proprietor of this hyperborean domain, is a neat mansion of dark stone, with a lawn spreading down to the shore of the inlet, and a pier, at which small vessels may draw up.

It being still early in the day, there were projects of excursionising. Boats were ordered to be lowered, and every one could do as he liked. The greater number were inclined for a walk across the hilly ground to Burra Fiord, to visit the dwelling-houses of the keepers who are connected with the light-house on the sea-girt rock at the northern extremity of Unst. The distance to the station was said to be three miles, others declared it to be good four miles, and this word good, I could gather, meant at least a mile more. Leaving the more adventurous to undertake this undefinable ramble, I chose to land with the Secretary and one of the Commissioners, for the purpose of paying our respects to the udaller of Buness, and asking him on board to dinner.

This was my first landing in Shetland. The scene was bleak, and the air as thin and chilly as might have been expected so near the sixty-first degree of north latitude. It was at this spot that Biot, the eminent French astronomer, resided in 1817, to make observations on the English arc of meridian, and determine the figure of the earth by the action of the pendulum. An upright stone, with an inscription, is pointed out as that to which his apparatus was attached. There was something pleasing in the idea that the place, with all its wildness, had been selected for an important scientific experiment. The late Mr Edmonston, uncle of the present worthy udaller, in whose time Biot paid his memorable visit, must have been a man of no ordinary kind. One of his fancies was so profound an admiration of the late Duke of Wellington, that he travelled all the way from Unst to London to see him, and, honoured with an interview, he became a favoured correspondent of the Duke. The present Mr Edmonston entertained us with an account of this incident in the family history, and shewed us a bundle of carefully preserved letters, written in the characteristic and well-known 'Field-marshal' style.

After a chat with Mr and Mrs Edmonston, we walked out to see the surroundings, and get a notion of the state of vegetation. I remark that trees are very much wanting for the sake of shelter, and the udaller, who has a laudable taste for improvement, points dolorously to the thin, withered shanks of some infant ashes and firs which he had planted within the walled policy. 'All dead,' I observe, with the proper degree of sympathy; 'but there is an artifice in planting trees. In order to get them to grow, you need to plant them close to each other, for the sake of mutual shelter and warmth; thin planting is worse than useless.' The udaller did not undervalue this hint; but, by way of practical answer, conducted us to a walled garden to notice the whimsicalities of a Shetland climate. The garden possessed a few apple and other trees, but not one of them shewed a green leaf above the top of the wall, the upper parts exposed to the blasts from the sea being scorched into the condition of a scavenger's broom. It passed through my mind that a single barrel of American apples would be ten times more to the purpose than all the fruit which could possibly be produced in Hialtland.

All were on board in time to dress for dinner at half-past six, at which hour the udaller came alongside in his boat, and was ceremoniously received on the quarter-deck. As we were to have a guest of this distinction, everything was ordered to be in the best style. One of the privileges of the commodore is to settle the bill of fare, and prescribe the wines and liqueurs that are to be used. After some cogitation with the steward on these important particulars, I issued the following *menu:* Mock turtle-soup, salmon, fillets of haddocks, dressed calf's-head, curried chicken, corned beef, greengage tart, cabinet-pudding, and savoury omelette; which, considering that we were lying in a northern voe fully three hundred miles from shops, was not bad. With the wine, walnuts, and other trifles on the table, and Philip as a faithful Ganymede ministerially at call, things went so merrily on that the early troubles of the week were forgotten. A facetious Commissioner told his drollest stories; another sang the *Bonnie House of Airlie* with uncommon dramatic effect; other melodists obligingly contributed to the general amusement; and from the udaller we received some particulars concerning the state of affairs in Shetland.

CHAPTER II.

SUNDAY, *July* 28.—A tranquil morning, at anchor in Balta Sound. All is hushed on board the *Pharos*. The crew is at rest; and Milo, grown somewhat obese, lies stretched out on the well-scrubbed deck. We hear no sound in our cabins but the low gurgling ripple of the water on the exterior of the vessel. The weather is still dull, and the sky overcast; but the drizzle has ceased, and there is a prospect of a tolerably pleasant walk to the parish church of Unst, which is spoken of as being little more than a mile distant in the direction of Burra Fiord. We see the road to it across the open heath, for roads, under the inspiration of an act of parliament, are beginning to make their appearance in these remote islands.

After breakfast, I am waited on by Captain Graham, to propose that divine service should be performed on board— say at a quarter to eleven o'clock, to allow time for afterwards going to church, if the Commissioners are disposed to go ashore. The service is to take place, as is customary, in the saloon, where the whole ship's company are to assemble. As commodore, I am expected to undertake the office of chaplain.

A few minutes before the appointed time, the steward spreads the Commissioners' flag on the table, and on it lays a large Bible, with which is bound up a printed prayer by the late Rev. Dr Brunton of Edinburgh, which, imperfect as I think in several particulars, I supplement from the *Book of Common Prayer*. At the sounding of the ship's bell, the whole company, in naval uniform, with Bibles in their hands, enter the saloon, and are accommodated with seats. The assemblage was decent and devout, and not a little interesting. The effect was considerably heightened by all singing the 100th Psalm, the tune of which was raised in proper style by a young gentleman, son of the Secretary, whom we had the pleasure of having with us. The service occupied about half an hour, after which all the party but myself went ashore to church. I had to refrain from going with them on account of the peculiar chilliness of the air, which seemed to pierce through me and cause a tendency to shivering. Left alone at the fireside in the saloon, I spent the forenoon with such solacement as could be gathered from a well-stocked library.

On deck at two o'clock, I see, by means of a field-glass, the people from the church dispersing over the bare slopes of the island to their several homes. Our party, which is approaching the boat, where it lies at the small quay near Buness, I observe, is recruited by two strangers, with whom an acquaintanceship had been made at church, and who were invited on board to luncheon. They prove to be two men of science out on an exploratory expedition, their chief object being to dredge for varieties of hitherto unknown shells on these wild northern shores. It is curious that, go where one will, he falls in with persons who know something of him, or with whom there is some bond of intimacy. One of the gentlemen in question knew my brother while he resided in London, and I had met the brother of the other several years ago in Dublin. An agreeable conversation accordingly ensued on matters of scientific and social concern. The two conchologists had not been very successful in their researches, in consequence of the bad weather, and they intended soon to depart, in order to be in time for the approaching meeting of the British Association. I ventured to hope that the sermon which the party had that day heard delivered at the parish church had been quite satisfactory; all spoke of it with more approbation than of the church itself, which, they said, looked as if it had not been swept or dusted for years.

One, however, should not expect to find here the trim order in which things are kept in populous and wealthy communities. Unst, like most other parts of Shetland, is at present experiencing an excessive pressure of local rates. Formerly, the poor used to get only two or three shillings a year for clothes, and were sent adrift from house to house for subsistence. But the new poor-law has changed all that. The udaller informed us that the poor-rates on his property amount to four shillings and tenpence per pound per annum on his valued rent, and that, after paying other public burdens, he does not get more than half his nominal rental. Probing the matter of rates, I learned that there was as yet no poor-house in Shetland to test the applications of paupers, and act as a stimulus to exertion : wherefore, as I hinted, there did not appear to be anything to prevent the whole rental of the islands from being diverted to the maintenance of the poor. Throughout the country, a middle class can scarcely be said to have grown up. There are proprietors, and a vast number of small tenants who pay their rent mostly in fish; to procure which the male inhabitants go to sea, and hang about the curing-stations, while the duty of attending to the land and to work generally, falls, in a great measure, to the share of the women—a system of social economics which seldom comes to any good. In a few places, the modern system of husbandry has been introduced with good effect; cottages have been pulled down, and their impoverished inhabitants got rid of, the land so cleared being thrown into farms of reasonable extent; but elsewhere, everything, as far as I could learn, is on a rude, primitive type. In some sheltered valleys there are, I was told, good crops under a proper rotation, which are aided by the long daylight from May to July, when absolute darkness even at midnight is unknown.

Monday, July 29.—The scene suddenly shifts. At half-past six o'clock, the anchor is heaved, steam is raised, and at seven the *Pharos* is pursuing its way out of Balta Sound, and once more facing the open sea.

'Well, commodore, where are we bound for now?' said one of the gentlemen on board, ascending to the gangway over the chart-room.

'We are,' I replied, 'going northward round the Scaw of Unst, in order to have a look at the light-house on the Mickle Flugga: as for landing at it, that, I fear, will be impossible, for there is still a heavy sea on; but we shall at all events shew ourselves to the keepers, and see some fine scenery in passing along the coast.'

The starting of the vessel, and the intelligence that we were going round by the Flugga, brought all the party on deck, and eyes were eagerly turned to the jagged, iron-bound coast along which we were driving. Both from the nature of the rocks and the violence of the sea, the coast of Shetland is generally abrupt, and we can observe that, from the more precipitous parts, large masses, after being undermined, have slid down and been engulfed in the ocean. The rocky structure of Unst is rich in chromate of iron, an article which, until lately, was quarried to a considerable extent, and exported by Mr Edmonston; competition from foreign countries has unfortunately ruined this valuable trade, and at present some thousands of tons remain unsaleable at a remunerating price. The stoppage of this branch of industry has of course limited the already too scanty means of employment on the island. The rocky shore, however, if not commercially productive, is at least strikingly picturesque, and would afford some fine studies for the marine artist.

Approaching Burra Fiord, we come in sight of two dark protuberances in the sea, at the distance of about two miles from land. On the larger of the two, which is nearest the shore, the light-house we are in quest of has been built. As these unshapely islets are out of the line of ordinary navigation, the planting of a light-house on one of them appears to be of doubtful utility. The work, it is proper to say, was not undertaken by the Commissioners until they were urged to do so by government during the progress of the Russian War, when a British squadron was expected to cruise in these northern latitudes. The history of the building of the light-house on the Mickle Flugga, as the larger islet is termed, would be as full of feats of daring and ingenuity as that of the tower of Skerryvore. The islet rises to a height of two hundred feet from the water, and is so rugged and precipitous as to be accessible only by steps cut in the southern or lowest side. On the summit, and overhanging the northern cliff, stands the light-house, a tower fifty feet high, surrounded by a wall, within which are embraced rooms for the storage of coal, oil, and other articles, the whole of which are hoisted from the landing vessel by means of a windlass and species of railway fixed at a slope on the surface of the rock. The execution of the various works. including houses for the families of the keepers at Burra Fiord, of which we have a glimpse in passing, cost thirty-two thousand pounds. The expense of light-house maintenance is greatly increased by the erection being placed on a solitary reef or islet; for in this case, four keepers (three of whom must always be on duty) are required instead of two. There is also much expense for boats and boatmen, besides storage of provisions. Worst of all, the keepers are liable, from stress of weather, to be cut off for weeks from the mainland, and doomed to compulsory exile on the rock, long after the time they should be relieved. This seemed to be the condition of the keepers belonging to the light-house now under notice. The sea rolled towards the islet in long swelling waves, which broke in swirling surges against the only landing-place, and rendered our visit impracticable. This was not less a disappointment to us than to the three keepers, who, hoisting their flag in our honour as soon as we came in sight, watched with sorrowful interest the vessel standing off, and pursuing a course towards the channel which divides Unst from Yell. And so that strangely placed light-house, with its flag wildly fluttering in the wind, and its keepers wandering like disturbed spirits round its lofty outworks, was left behind in its dismal solitude—a thing to intrude on remembrance in the wakeful moments of night, when we think of these distant regions, and the inclemencies to which they are exposed.

On this memorable morning, which saw us compass the northern limits of the British Islands, breakfast was put off for half an hour, in order that we might sit down with comfort in the comparative tranquillity of a sheltered sound. With Unst and afterwards Fetlar on our left, and the large island of Yell on our right, the *Pharos* pursued its way undisturbed, and the further south we advanced, the weather continued to improve. By the ship's officers, Fetlar was described as being considerably cleared of its old cotter system, and transformed into pastoral farms of a modern type.

The island, I was informed, is one of those from which ponies of the small Shetland breed continue to be exported.

Doubling on our former course, we were abreast of Whalsay Skerries about noon; but again no landing could be effected on the outer skerry, or small rocky islet on which the light-house is placed. A boat, however, was able to reach the larger island, containing the houses for the families of the keepers. This station, which we inspected, is not satisfactory. Besides suffering from an imperfect supply of water, the dwellings are planted on an exposed brow overlooking the sea, and being unprotected by a surrounding wall, are open to all the storms that can blow. Who are responsible for this and some other defects which are prolific of constant outlay? Not the Commissioners of Northern Light-houses, but the Board of Trade, in the exercise of those powers of control given to it by the Merchant Shipping Act of 1854. As the Board sanctions the expenditure on light-houses from an imperial fund, the Commissioners are relieved from a dependence on mere surplus dues for the erection of new establishments. This plan, doubtless, works very advantageously as regards maritime interests; but as has been alluded to in 'My First Holiday,' the Board of Trade is apt at times, through a spirit of economy, to be a little too parsimonious. Wherefore, as at Whalsay, the want of surrounding walls to afford shelter to the dwellings, and often also that want of hand-rails in the steep staircases of the towers, which Commissioners of a certain age feel to be somewhat trying. It is commonly remarked that the Scottish light-house establishments of recent date for the most part poorly compare in point of substantiality and comfort with those of earlier origin, when the Commissioners were not subject to this kind of control.

Passing Noss Head, the vessel bore us into Bressay Sound, which separates the island of Bressay on the east from the mainland of Shetland on the west. On a prominent headland on our right stands Bressay light-house, which we are fortunately able to visit and inspect. Immediately afterwards, the *Pharos* steamed up the Sound to Lerwick, the capital of Shetland. In approaching it, we see, on a prominent knoll on our left, some modern buildings of tasteful architecture, the gift of Mr Anderson, a native of the town, and designed for an academy and retreat for a certain class of aged persons. Behind the knoll, in front of a finely-sheltered bay, we find Lerwick, built in a most irregular manner on the gentle declivity of a hill, with an eastern exposure. The most conspicuous feature in its character is that the houses nearest to us are built with their gables into or close upon the water, with intervening steps or slips of quay which lead to the main street, if so it can be called; for it is nothing more than an irregular lane, varying in breadth, but at the narrowest parts sufficiently wide to admit the passage of a cart. With lanes of lesser dimensions extending to the higher and more open parts of the town, and with buildings set down with little attention to regularity, there is altogether a foreign dash about Lerwick, or at least an air of novelty, according to our conceptions. There is one peculiarity deserving of special notice, and that is the fact of its thoroughfares being well paved all over with flagstones, as is the case with Genoa and Naples. For this comfort, it is doubtless indebted to the prevalence of that kind of stone in the neighbourhood, which is easily quarried in flat slabs for pavement. Why the outer fringe of buildings should be set down within sea-mark, is not commonly explained, and we are left to conjecture that this fashion of house-building has had something to do with the landing of articles without the formality of paying customs-duties.

Lerwick is not an old town; probably not older than the middle of the seventeenth century; the original capital of the country having been Scalloway, a decayed town, with the ruins of the infamous Earl Patrick's castle situated on the west side of the mainland, which, I am sorry to say, in spite of the best intentions, we had no opportunity of visiting. Although shewing symptoms of improvement—in particular, no want of variety in churches—Lerwick has obviously still to do a good deal to procure a character conformable with modern ideas of civic economy. In particular, its thoroughfares require widening; and it requires a hotel for the accommodation of those strangers who may be disposed to pay it a visit. I hope to hear that in these and some other matters it has made a start in advance.

While several of our party landed to visit Fort Charlotte, which commands the harbour, and could effectually protect the shipping, I proceeded with the sheriff of Wigtonshire to make some calls in the town. But we could not have done so at a more inopportune period. It was five o'clock in the afternoon; the mail-steamer for Granton, which was seen lying at anchor, was to depart at half-past six, and the whole community were engaged in writing their letters for the south. This is a serious affair, for there is a despatch only at intervals of several days; and what in these circumstances will not one do to avoid ceremonial interruptions? I am afraid our visit was inconvenient in more places than one; yet nothing could exceed the politeness with which we were received. If my limited experience is worth anything, it goes to verify the reputation which the Shetland gentry have acquired for their hospitable and kindly feelings. We extended our walk to Hayfield, a villa prettily situated, and with a fine look-out, at the distance of half a mile from the town. One of the objects of our intrusive calls was to offer invitations to dinner; and as a result, the Commissioners were favoured with the company of Mr Muir, the recently settled sheriff-substitute, and of one of the Messrs Hay, whose firm possesses the chief import and export trade of the place. It need hardly be said that the great article of export is dried white fish, chiefly ling and tusk, vast quantities of which are carried away annually for Spanish consumption. In preparation for these exports, piles of fish are seen stacked up along the coasts, to be sent with boats in due season to Lerwick. The exports generally of Shetland have been much increased in recent times by the introduction of steam-communication ; so much is this the case, that the prices of all native produce have risen, and the cost of articles of daily consumption at Lerwick does not, it is said, greatly differ from what it is at Edinburgh. One particular export deserves to be noticed ; I refer to those knitted woollen articles, which, for fineness and tastefulness, have obtained a wide celebrity. In the produce of these articles by hand-labour, there is manifested an extraordinary amount of feminine industry, which, it is to be hoped, meets with a fair reward. At my request, a young and skilled *tricoteuse* was sent on board to exhibit the knitted wares she had for sale, and she offered for inspection some shawls of remark-ably delicate texture, one of which I purchased to take home as a present. Knitting seems universal. Women of a humble class may be observed busy at this kind of work while engaged in carrying back-loads of peats into Lerwick, or when on their way to some sort of rural occupation.

In the course of conversation with our guests at dinner, I was curious to know how far the old Norwegian traditions and usages had disappeared before modern improvements, and learned that little of them remains, at least in Lerwick and its neighbourhood. Mr Hay expressed some regret that the once useful official, the Ranzelman, whose duties somewhat resembled those of a bailie and head-constable, had vanished along with the Fowdes, or aboriginal magistrates, of different degrees of importance : but it is not clear that the united action of a procurator-fiscal and a sheriff is either quite so cheap or so expeditious in composing differences as that of the Ranzelman of a former polity.

Talking of maritime matters, it was mentioned that two fishermen of Lerwick had just reported having seen a large whale, probably worth a thousand pounds, floating about at sea without an owner. I asked 'why the fishermen had not tried to secure so valuable a prize—it might have made their fortune.' For the explanations in reply I was not prepared. 'If the dead whale in question had been towed to land, it would have been taken possession of by the receiver of wreck, without perhaps giving so much as thanks to the poor men who took the trouble to bring it in.' The provisions of the Merchant Shipping Act, as regards the saving of wreckage, though of undoubted value in preventing the plunder of property thrown on the shore, are, after all, not the perfection of human wisdom. It cannot be considered a very judicious thing to discourage fishermen from securing waifs, such as dead whales, which, left to themselves, would disappear on the face of the deep, and be of no use to anybody. How often are we taught that there is a possibility of being too 'sicker !'

On the principle of prevention being better than cure, the

establishment of a series of light-houses from the Pentland
Firth to Bressay Sound, has done more for the mariner in
this quarter than any laws that could be invented. Shipwreck on the coast of Orkney and Shetland is now of so
rare occurrence, that the inhabitants no longer speculate on
eking out a living by what the sea may casually send them,
and therefore rely more distinctly on regular industry. The
same thing, however, may be said as regards the east and
west coast of the mainland of Scotland ; long tracts of
which—as, for example, from the Sound of Jura to Cape
Wrath—are now lighted almost like a street. I remember
a party of Commissioners facetiously talking of a letter that
had been some years ago received from a gentleman, praying
for a charitable contribution to a particular district, the
grounds of application being that the inhabitants of the
neighbourhood had seriously suffered in their means of
livelihood by the establishment of a light-house !

Dinner-party broke up at ten—for the *Pharos* keeps good
hours—and bidding our Lerwick guests farewell, see them
handsomely off in a six-oared boat for the not far-distant
shore. We all turn in and the ship lies quietly at anchor
for the night.

CHAPTER III.

AS a result of some reading and conversation during the last two or three days, I note the following particulars concerning the history of Shetland, Zetland, or Hialtland, as it is variously called.

It is difficult to determine whether the Romans were acquainted with Shetland. It is certain, however, that the emperor Claudius, about the year 43 of our era, visited what the Roman writers call the ' Orcades,' whence the modern term Orkney. Virgil speaks of the power of Augustus being extended ' ultima Thule '—to the furthest Thule ; but where was this Thule? is the question. Was Orkney Thule, or was it Shetland? A modern writer speculates on the island of Foula being Thule ; all we have to do being to substitute *Th* for *F*, in order to make the two words resemble each other. I fear that this easy way of getting over the difficulty will not answer. However, it is open to any one to point out the true Thule, and until that is done we may take the liberty of assigning Virgil's designation to Shetland.

The earliest inhabitants of the Orkney and Shetland islands are usually spoken of as being the Picts. But then comes the perplexing question, who were the Picts? If ever there were such a people, of whom stories are told that seem to be little better than fabulous invention, they were assuredly, as concerns Orkney and Shetland, not a Celtic race ; because there is not a trace of Celtic ancestry in these islands, nor of Celtic terms applied to localities. Looking to existing antiquities, of which I will have to say something in due season, it would appear that the early inhabitants of these islands—more particularly Orkney—were a branch of the same people who occupied England in ages before the intrusion of the Celts. Be this as it may, there can be no doubt that the occupants of the islands during the middle ages were of Scandinavian lineage—colonists, in fact, from Norway—spoke the Norse tongue, and were governed by Norse chiefs, who with Norse laws and usages affected a certain degree of independence. The medieval history of Orkney and Shetland has accordingly little connection with the history of either England or Scotland. It is a history properly belonging to that of Norway.

In looking to the Scotland of the present day consolidated into a harmonious whole, we are apt to forget that it did not, even as lately as the twelfth century, comprehend the Hebrides on the west, or the Orkney and Shetland islands on the north of the country. Of these various islands the kings of Norway made themselves masters in the ninth century. In 875, Harold Harfager, king of Norway, wrested the whole from native chiefs, and for centuries afterwards they were under the rule of Jarls or Earls, as also bishops and other functionaries, deriving authority from the Norwegian monarchs. We hear little good of the Lords and Jarls of the Isles, who were incessantly fighting with, and robbing and killing each other. As a specimen, take one ·of them named Sigurd, who became Earl of Orkney and Zetland about 915, a ruffian who well deserved the fate recorded of him. Having, with a body of mounted followers, completed a victory over certain chiefs in the north of Scotland, he directed each horseman to suspend the head of a fallen enemy from his saddle. He carried one of these hideous trophies himself. It was the head of a knight, from a tooth in which, Sigurd, in suddenly leaping his horse, received so severe a wound in the calf of the leg that the part mortified, and he died soon after.

Intelligible Scottish history, as we all know, opens in the reign of Alexander III., when that monarch, partly by a victory over Hacon, king of Norway, at Largs, 1263, and subsequently by a negotiation with Magnus, Hacon's son and successor, in which he agreed to pay an annual quit-rent, established the authority of the Scottish crown over the Hebrides, 1266. That, then, is the date of the annexation of these western islands to Scotland. The quit-rent, known as the annual of Norway, was never regularly paid, and at length there were such heavy arrears due, that Christiern, king of Denmark, successor of the old Norwegians, issued threatening denunciations against Scotland. Money being a scarce article in these times, compliance with Christiern's demand was plainly impracticable. What followed is an amusing instance of the way in which the tables may be turned on a clamorous creditor. When matters between Denmark and Scotland were on the point of explosion, certain friends of both parties happily fell upon a method of settlement : Let Christiern give his daughter Margaret in marriage to James III., the young king of Scotland; abolish the annual; cancel the debt; and as a handsome thing, let the princess have a dowry of sixty thousand florins. On these terms, settled by treaty at Copenhagen in 1468—and which I am astonished that Christiern agreed to—the marriage of James and Margaret took place. According to the bargain, James was to have ten thousand florins cash down with the princess, and for the remaining fifty thousand the Orkney Islands were to be assigned in pledge. After all, Christiern could not manage to pay the stipulated ten thousand. He said he could give no more than two thousand, and James might take the Shetland islands in pledge for the remaining eight thousand. They were taken accordingly. It does not appear that the king of Denmark ever paid a shilling of the promised dowry. Certainly, he failed to redeem the two pledges which he had given. And so, for want of an insignificant sum, Denmark had to relinquish both groups of islands, which, to make things secure, were irrevocably annexed by act of parliament to the Scottish crown, 1470.

From that period, the Orkney and Shetland islands followed the fortunes of Scotland, but for many years they were the prey of a series of rapacious court favourites, who exceeded all the ordinary rights of feudal superiors. The most extravagant and oppressive of these autocrats was Patrick Stewart, Earl of Orkney, son of Earl Robert, who was a natural son of James V. The conduct of Earl Patrick resembled more that of an unprincipled Eastern pasha than a royal viceroy or commissioner. Dwelling in state at his castle of Scalloway in Shetland, or his palace at Kirkwall in Orkney, he moved about with a large band of armed retainers, made laws to suit his own selfish purposes, extorted fines and confiscated the lands of proprietors, and cruelly pressed fishermen and artificers into his service, whom he forced to labour for him without fee or reward. For his petty tyrannies, the earl might have escaped the vengeance of the law, but his assumption of regal powers could not be overlooked. Summoned to answer for his crimes, he was confined first as a prisoner in Edinburgh Castle, and afterwards, for greater security, in the Castle of Dumbarton. In this last-mentioned place of confinement he had the imprudence and audacity to induce his natural son, Robert, a youth of twenty-two years of age, to proceed to Kirkwall, and there hold out the castle against the royal power, until he, the earl, should effect his escape. Besieged by a force under the Earl of Caithness on behalf of the crown, the castle was resolutely maintained by Robert for the space of two months; but at length, September 29, 1614, was surrendered by a retainer, Patrick Halcro, on condition that his own life should be saved. Robert and five of his company were tried and hanged at Edinburgh, January 1615. A few days later (February 6), Earl Patrick was beheaded at the Cross in the same city—the spectacle of an earl, cousin of the king, led out to execution, being one of the memorable events in a reign noted for its ghastly public tragedies. Stripped of everything, a son of the earl was fain to beg an alms from parish kirk-sessions. The whole history of this family of Stewarts is so full of romantic and tragic qualities, that one wonders why it has never been fully and popularly narrated. The ordinary histories of Scotland barely allude to the subject.*

The next oppressor of the islanders was Sir James Stewart of Kilsyth, afterwards Lord Ochiltree, in the capacity of farmer-general. In 1643, William, Earl of Morton, was granted the jurisdictions and royal rents of the islands, and under his chamberlains there were fresh forms of exaction. The Morton family being confirmed in its rights and privileges in 1742, was able to dispose of them in 1766 for the sum of £60,000 to Sir Lawrence Dundas, ancestor of the present Earl of Zetland, who now enjoys this insular heritage, in which is embraced the right of drawing

---

* Inquirers may consult an ably edited body of documents, *Oppressions of the Islands of Orkney and Zetland*, presented to the Maitland Club by David Balfour, Esq. of Balfour and Trenabie; also Pitcairn's *Criminal Trials :* and Chambers's *Domestic Annals of Scotland.*

rents and duties of various kinds, with patronage of churches, &c.

The primary blunder of the crown which has led to no end of extortions and litigations, was the assigning of these islands as a squeezable inheritance to a set of worthless courtiers. It seems to have been a leading object with these personages to alter the holding of the lands throughout the islands from *udal* to *feudal* tenure. According to the old udal holding derived from the Norwegian system, the proprietor enjoyed his lands in absolute freehold heritage, with or without the intervention of written title. Earl Patrick's policy consisted in compelling the udallers to receive feudal investiture from himself as superior, and in his time this change was effected on a large scale. Since that period, most of the landed possessions in Orkney and Shetland have been brought under feudal holding, such as is common elsewhere in Scotland; proprietors, generally, however, still being familiarly styled udallers.* One of the wrongs which the udallers have had to complain of is the exaction of *scatt*, an old Danish land-tax, and also the payment of the modern British land-tax, levied from the same properties. In the scatt, which has been adjudged to be of the character of a feu-duty, is now included the *wattle*, a petty tax formerly paid to the Fowd, or local magistrate. I am sorry that I have neither time nor space to go deeper into this intricate subject; and can only state it as my

---

* About 1823, old deeds of udal tenure were sold as curiosities at book-stalls in Edinburgh at a shilling apiece. They consisted of dingy pieces of vellum scarcely six inches square, with a seal in the corner, and were dated at Bergen in Norway. How these documents should have been brought away from Orkney and Shetland, and how they came to this low pass, instead of being deposited among public records, I am unable to explain. The circumstance is distinctly in my recollection.

impression, from a perusal of various works, that the landed proprietors of Orkney and Shetland have first and last been very shamefully treated.

Whether as being nearer to the mainland of Scotland, or from other circumstances, Orkney has been fortunate in coming in for a greater share of public favour than Shetland. James III. erected Kirkwall into a royal burgh in 1486; but Shetland had less reason to repine at the granting of this distinction than to feel aggrieved at having no share with Orkney in parliamentary representation until the Reform Act of 1832, although both formed one county. Dr Edmondston writes sorely on this mark of political injustice and degradation, seeing, as he says, that 'the inhabitants of Zetland are extremely loyal, and they pay without a murmur every tax which is imposed on them; nor does any part of the empire, for its population, supply so many sailors to the navy.' * As regards redress for this and other wrongs, the udallers perhaps fell into the mistake of not being sufficiently clamorous.

It appears that the principal families in the islands are descended from Scottish gentlemen who settled in the seventeenth and early part of the eighteenth century; there being few who claim Norwegian descent. The Norse tongue, which, according to Brand, still lingered among the people when he visited Orkney and Shetland in 1700, has been completely superseded by English. Brand's visit was an historical incident. He was one of a deputation from the General Assembly to settle the Presbyterian Church polity in the islands, in virtue of the Revolution Settlement. His account of what he saw and heard on the occasion is

---

* *View of the Ancient and Present State of the Zetland Islands*, by Arthur Edmondston, M.D. ; 2 vols. 8vo, 1809.

exceedingly amusing. He gravely tells us that there were still witches in the islands, and that 'not above forty or fifty years ago, almost every family had a Brownie, or evil spirit so called, which served them, and to whom they gave sacrifice.' We likewise hear of various superstitious usages ; some of which have a hold on the popular fancy even till our own times. Dr Edmondston mentions that there was still a belief in lucky and unlucky occurrences; as, for example : 'If a man tread on the tongs in the morning, or be asked where he is going, he need not go to the fishing that day. Certain names must not be mentioned while they are setting their lines, especially the minister and the cat.' It would appear that a belief in the cure of scrofula by the royal touch still holds its ground in Shetland. This fact is learned from the Statistical Account of the parish of Mid and South Yell, written in 1841. As, however, the royal touch is impracticable, a substitute is found in touching a few half-crowns of the coinage of Charles I. ; 'there being few localities in Shetland in which a living evidence is not to be found of one said to have been "cured by the coin."' If disposed to laugh at this, we have to keep in mind that on the 30th of March 1712, Queen Anne touched as many as two hundred persons 'for the evil;' and that Swift and other learned persons of his time believed—or affected to believe—in the efficacy of this nonsensical ceremonial. The lower class of Shetlanders are therefore only a hundred and fifty years— if so much—behind the best English society as regards this superstition. Their notion that touching certain coins is of equal value with the royal touch, is perhaps derived from the circumstance of patients having received a small gold coin, called a 'Touch-piece,' when dismissed from the royal presence.

CHAPTER IV

TUESDAY, *July* 30.—As previously arranged, the *Pharos* got up steam at seven o'clock, at which early hour we bade good-bye to Lerwick, while the thin blue smoke of the peat-fires from the chimneys of the irregularly-built town ascended in the morning air. Our way was southward down Bressay Sound, keeping so near to the mainland as to take the narrow channel between it and the island of Mousa. Without going out of our course, I was anxious on my own part as well as on that of others to see the tower of Mousa, ordinarily called Burgh-Mousa, about which there has been no little discussion among antiquaries.

Without being much of an archæologist, I may presume to say that the Shetland group of islands does not exhibit any memorials referrible to a very remote historical period— at least, none of any moment. Its antiquities are principally medieval, or dating from probably the seventh or eighth century, when the natives were exposed to the harassing predatory incursions of the Norsemen, previous to the conquest by Harold Harfager. The old towers scattered about Shetland and the north of Scotland, which are usually spoken of as having been built by the Picts, are all similar in character, and peculiar in construction. We had a glance at the remains of one of them situated on an island in a loch near Lerwick, and now we were to see another which, by means of recent repairs, is singularly complete, and certainly so interesting as to be worthy of deliberate inspection.

In going southward down the channel, which is about a mile wide, the tower of Mousa made its appearance on our left, and stopping the vessel for a few minutes, a boat-load of us went ashore to pay it a visit. It occupies a knoll close upon the rocky sea-beach, from which materials for its construction had been taken. The whole fabric is composed of flat slabs of clay slate, which have been easily piled together in a compact mass without the aid of mortar. In exterior figure, the tower is round, inclining inwards about half-way up, and then bulging out near the top. Near the foundation, its circumference is 158 feet, and it measures about 40 feet in height. On the side next the sea, there is a doorway, and that is the only exterior aperture. If there were ever any door-posts, they have disappeared; it is feasibly conjectured, however, that instead of employing a door, the inmates had, on emergencies, built up the opening, for which there is an abundance of loose materials at hand. Entering the doorway, we find the wall sixteen feet thick, and looking upwards, feel as if we were at the bottom of a well, for the circular interior has no flooring, and the top is open to the sky. Opposite the doorway, there is an entrance to a passage and stair, which wind upwards, within the thickness of the wall, to the summit of the building. At different places, there are recesses, or galleries, leading off from the stair, lighted by apertures to the interior; such dismal holes being all that we find in the way of apartments. It is customary to speak of an outer and inner wall; but the two walls, if we so distinguish them, are so firmly bound together by the stair and otherwise, as to afford a united resistance to assault. Obviously, the structure was used as a retreat in case of attack from foreign enemies, against whom missiles could be showered down from the species of battlement formed by the top of the well-knit walls. According to tradition, the tower of Mousa was occupied by

Erland, a Norwegian Jarl, about 1154, when it successfully endured a siege that was undertaken to recover a runaway lady; but how any lady could have found accommodation in such miserable quarters it is difficult to conjecture. The Society of Scottish Antiquaries deserves thanks for having repaired this fine memorial of a former state of society in

Tower of Burgh-Mousa, from a photograph by Mr Marwick.

Shetland. In sailing away, we see the fragment of a similar building on the coast of the mainland immediately opposite.

Holding on southward, we, in little more than an hour, reach Sumburgh Head, when we may be said to be amidst the scenery so faithfully described in the *Pirate;* and viewing it as classic ground, I may be excused for going over it somewhat leisurely. Sir Walter Scott tells us that it was as a guest of the Commissioners of the Northern

Light-houses that he visited Shetland, in their armed yacht.
in the summer of 1814; and that, as the nature of the
important business which occupied the Commissioners was
connected with the amusement of visiting the leading
objects of a traveller's curiosity, he was enabled to store up
recollections, and to hear of circumstances, out of which he
afterwards constructed his fictitious narrative.   Here were
we, successors of these Commissioners, engaged in a similar
duty, and going over the same ground, but with the superior
advantage of being in a steamer, which, threading its way
into voes, could set us down with the precision of a carriage
driving up to a doorway.

At Sumburgh Head we were in the Roost or tide-flow
noticed by the novelist for its impetuosity and danger to
mariners.   On the present occasion, the sea was calmer than
anything we had yet experienced; and rounding the cape,
we steered into West Voe, and cast anchor opposite the low
neck of land on which stands the ruin of Jarlshof.   At
this point, we went on shore to walk to the light-house, a
distance of a mile and a half, over which there is a constant
ascent.   The day was fine, the first on which we had any
sunshine, and the walk was a relief from the confinement
on shipboard.   Jarlshof consists of the gables and other
walls of what had been once a spacious dwelling with out-
houses, possessing an outlook to the voe in front, and
having some garden-ground behind.   Jarlshof—pronounced
Yarlshof, and signifying Earl's House—is said to have
been a residence of Robert Stewart, Earl of Orkney, father
of the. cruel Earl Patrick.   The whole ruin, which is
plain and devoid of inscription, was seen in a moment, and
there was nothing to detain us from our walk, which was
partly along a road to a farm establishment that lay on

our line of route. Near to Jarlshof, the proprietor of
Sumburgh is building a new mansion, which will command a view over the level sandy tract and the sea on
each side of the peninsula which terminates in the bold
cape on the south. In twos and threes, we are to be
supposed as jogging on our way up the long grassy slope

Ruins of Jarlshof, from a photograph by Mr Marwick.

towards this prominent headland. At length the light-
house is reached, and then begins the climb to the top of
the tower, whence we have a magnificent prospect of sea
and land, rendered lively by the flight of numerous gulls
and other birds which inhabit the crevices of the cliff
beneath. From the top of Sumburgh light-house is seen in
clear weather the light of North Ronaldshay, in Orkney, and,
I believe, from few other points are the two groups of islands
visible from each other. It is only by an actual visit that

one learns how thoroughly the Shetland islands are disconnected with those of Orkney—the association being political and nothing more—and also how the Shetlanders still speak of going to Scotland, as if it were to them a kind of foreign country. A young woman, with whom we conversed at Sumburgh Head, mentioned to us that ' she had never been in Scotland;' her furthest stretch southwards having been only as far as the Pentland Skerries, within sight of Caithness.

From the elevated spot we had reached, forming the southern extremity of the parish of Dunrossness, the scene was most picturesque towards the north-west, for in this direction we had Quendale Bay bounded by Fitful Head ; and more remotely, lying in solitary grandeur in the ocean between Shetland and Orkney, the lofty island of Foula, which, above all things, we had been told to try to visit. The sight of Quendale Bay reminded me that it was at Quendale House, the residence of Malcolm Sinclair, that the Duke of Medina Sidonia found a temporary and hospitable retreat on quitting Fair Isle after his shipwreck. Here, says Sir Robert Sibbald, in his *Description of the Zetland Isles,* the duke remained till a ship was ready to take him away. ' Imagining the people did admire him, he made his interpreter ask Malcolm Sinclair of Quendale if ever he had seen such a man. To which Malcolm, in broad Scots (unintelligible to the interpreter), replied : " Farcie on that face, I have seen many prettier men hanging on the Burrow-moor." '

The estate of Sumburgh appeared to be under an improved system of farming. The sheep in enclosed parks were of a superior breed, and in good condition. At the farmsteading, through which we had to pass, I had the curiosity to examine a turret-like structure, somewhat of the Pictish tower type. It proved to be a kiln of a kind common in the islands for drying corn, but which are now, in many instances, disused.

Loitering on the shore, under the ruins of Jarlshof, until all the party return from their official inspection, a conversation takes place on things in general and the future proceedings for the day in particular.

'The commodore had better let us hear his mind as to the route,' says one. 'I would like to know what he thinks about Foula,' says another, evidently trusting in the efficacy of the hint.

'Well, gentlemen,' I reply, with the gravity suitable to my high function, 'this is a serious matter, and I have been thinking over it for some time. I will give you my view of the affair. In the first place, we have finished off the Shetland light-houses, and our next move is to Orkney. On consulting the printed programme in your pockets, you will observe that our anchorage for the night is to be Otterswick Bay, in the island of Sanday. In point of fact, we could not do better. If we reach Otterswick by eight o'clock in the evening, we shall do excellently, for the sea is now so calm that it will make no sort of difference whether we dine while sailing or at anchor. Now, having a long day still before us, why not bend a little northward to have a look at the western shores of Shetland, where there are as yet no light-houses? I understand there has been some official correspondence as to the propriety of establishing one on the Vie Skerries, near Papa Stour, and also one somewhere about Skelda Ness, bearing north-west on the Bay of Scalloway. I say, therefore, why not, when we are thus far, take a look in that direction? Our doing so may be useful to the service. Whether we can touch at Foula, will depend on tides and other circumstances, of which the captain will be the best judge. If we can do so conveniently, I have no objections. And I may add, as perhaps not a bad reason for calling at the island, that the steward hints he is getting short of eggs and poultry, and at a small cost a good stock may be laid in.' This line of argument was complimented for its perspicacity. I was told that I had exhausted the subject. There was not another word to be said.

There was a disposition to be off, but a number had not yet arrived. The Secretary, who has much to do in making up notes on such occasions, was still absent; and so was one of our guests, Mr Marwick, Town-clerk of Edinburgh, who, with the aid of an apparatus, fixed to the top of a tall tripod, was taking a photograph of Erick's Steps, the cleft in the rock by which, the novelist informs us, the inhabitants of Jarlshof were wont for any purpose to seek access to the foot of the precipice beneath the headland. At last all have reached the attending boat, except Milo, which has for an hour been chasing rabbits among the sand-heaps, and seems unwilling to abandon his sport. The mate is despatched on a mission to get hold of him; and ultimately, after a good deal of whistling and scolding, he is persuaded to return from his scamper. Getting him securely into the boat, where he modestly settles down under the cross-benches of the oarsmen, we shove off from this interesting locality, and in a few minutes we are again placed on the deck of the *Pharos*.

The captain, with whom I had immediate conference, declared that, as regards tide and everything else, it would be quite practicable to touch at Foula. 'Let us, however,' said I, 'stretch the compasses across the chart, and measuring the distance, calculate when we shall reach our anchorage at Otterswick.' This was a simple matter. It was seen that, after giving an hour to Foula, we could be at Otterswick about eight in the evening, the hour on which I had speculated.

The vessel, thereupon, is steered in a north-westerly course, to bring us in front of Fitful Head, which rises in a slope so much more abrupt from the water-edge than the angle of repose, that its crumbling strata of sand-flag are to all appearance constantly sliding down into the sea in a state of disintegration. With eyes turned towards this renowned headland, we with some interest observe a number of boats out on a cruise for white-fish. For a minute, the vessel stops in its career, and the waste steam hissing off is a sufficient signal for such boatmen to approach as have anything to dispose of. Right and left, what a competition to be first in reaching this unexpected market! The boat that gains the race is manned by three roughly-clad fishermen, who, on being asked what newly-caught fish they had, hold up three large tusk, which the cook and his assistant instantly clutch by the gills, and, in return, to complete the bargain, the steward tosses half-a-crown, which is received with a grin of perfect satisfaction. Again we are on our appointed course—the three fish, destined to figure in successive *menus*, being for some time objects of interest in a culinary, if not natural history point of view, lying in a tub at the entrance to the cook's galley. All the boats, of which we had just seen a specimen, are here, as elsewhere in Shetland, on the old Norwegian model. They are light, shallow, and pointed at each end, ready for being turned in any direction by a dexterous handling of the oars. Eminently adapted to the wants of a people of small means and simple habits, they fall far short of what is required for the *Haaf* or deep-sea fishing on the scale demanded by enlarged modern requirements; and unfortunately, there is scarcely a season in which some of these small boats are not lost with all their crews. But how are these disasters to be averted? A land-owner in Shetland told me that he had made an attempt to employ fishermen on wages to fish with a decked vessel, but the experiment had not succeeded to his satisfaction, and was about to be given up.

Fitful Head is passed, and holding out to sea, we watch the gradual development of Foula, as it emerges from the distant haze, massive and solitary on the face of the deep. Its distance is about thirty-five miles north-west of Sumburgh Head, and eighteen miles directly west of the parish of Walls, to which it is considered to belong. Whatever be the theory as to its ecclesiastical and civil status, Foula is practically a thing by itself, and out of the way of general traffic; as little is known about it, as if it were an island in the Southern Pacific. Unknown to the world, the world is unknown to it; at all events, its thread of connection with the ongoings of society is so slender as to be hardly recognisable. There was not one on board who had ever landed on Foula, or seen it nearer than at a distance of thirty miles. The curiosity was, on all hands, correspondingly great to see what it was like. On approaching it, we almost felt ourselves rising into the character of discoverers.

It is a blessing to mariners, that go where they will among the British islands, they are provided with a faithful guide in the numerous charts issued by the Admiralty. On these, the result of careful hydrographic survey, the soundings are marked in figures, and sunk rocks and strong tidal currents are also plainly indicated. The *Pharos*, as may be supposed, is provided with a full assortment of these valuable charts, one of which, appropriate to the sea that is traversed, is always at hand on the gangway, to be readily appealed to by the captain or mate in charge. Examining the chart on the present occasion, there was an assurance of deep water all round Foula, except at the Have de Grind Rocks, which lie about three miles to the east, and shew their presence by boiling surges that are observable at a considerable distance. But these dangerous reefs were not in our course. Steering right up to the island, on its southern side, the vessel was not stopped till within half a mile of the shore.

At this point, we had a capital view of the island, which, from a low rocky shore, swelled gracefully upwards to some enclosed arable land, whence the ground ascended rapidly to a height, as marked by the chart, of 1369 feet above sea-level. Such is the southern aspect of Foula; but, as we afterwards found, the appearance is very different on the west and north, where the single mountain of which it may be said to be composed is worn away to a bold and magnificent precipice. The sudden apparition of a large steamer seemed to spread a degree of consternation among the inhabitants. We could see the women making off from their scattered dwellings to the higher grounds, where they stood in groups watching our proceedings. The men were more courageous, yet they looked as if they were not quite sure of us, and perhaps, as occurred elsewhere not long ago in a part of Shetland, associated us with terror-striking traditions of 'the press-gang.' A boat being lowered, our party proceeded to the shore, and effected a landing at some broken masses of rock, up which we scrambled to dry land, holding out presents of newspapers to the natives, and beckoning on them to come forward. In this, however, they manifested great reluctance. One or two men shyly accepted our gifts; but nothing at first could induce the females to approach, and some of them positively fled to a greater distance. We saw no children, and afterwards learned that they had been hidden in the holes and corners of the dwellings.

The sheriff of Wigtonshire, with a handful of newspapers, and using many earnest as well as kindly solicitations, was the first to be successful in quelling the female panic. The women, in small parties, ventured to come near us, and were told that we merely wanted to see the island, and to know how the people lived. Confidence being established, we proceeded to make an inspection of several clusters of dwellings and the small patches of cultured ground in their vicinity. In our walk thither, we could not but view with sorrow the process of scarifying the pastoral part of the land, in order to carry away the turf for fuel, and also for material to enrich the scraps of ground under crops of bear, oats, and potatoes. To such an extent is this ruinous practice carried, that much of the grassy slope facing the sea is reduced to the condition of a stony waste; and what the inhabitants are to do when all the superficial layer of turf is gone, is more than I can tell, unless it be to suffer downright starvation.

Any one who has seen the hovels occupied by the poorer inhabitants of Skye and other western islands, can have no difficulty in understanding the domestic architecture of Foula —lowly thatched dwellings with a peat-fire in the middle of the clay-floor, from which the smoke, after hanging about the dingy interior, escapes through a hole in the roof. The first dwelling we entered had a cow house as a sort of side-apartment, and in a lesser den in the passage from the door we found two calves. As there was a pig-house outside, we concluded that the establishment was of a somewhat high order. The live-stock in the other dwellings was, as far as we could see, less extensive. As a kind of excuse for our intrusion, we made some inquiry as to poultry, and hinted that eggs might find a good customer; but there was evidently a scarcity of anything saleable. All the provisions

Domestic Architecture of Foula.

which the steward could forage were a couple of hens, purchased from an old crone at the moderate price of eighteenpence.

We could recognise no difference in the dress of the islanders from what we are accustomed to in the Hebrides, except in two particulars. The women have handkerchiefs or small shawls thrown over the head, and tied loosely under the chin; and both men and women wear a species of sandals called 'rivelins' instead of shoes. I had seen the humbler class of women at Lerwick with the same kind of foot-covering. The sandals are pieces of hide secured by strings drawn together, after the picturesque fashion of the peasantry of the Abruzzi, such as Italian artists have a fancy for delineating. To render the tread soft, straw or wool is introduced below the foot; and some artifice of that kind would, I think, be required in walking with skin-sandals over the rough, scarified land of Foula.

In the article of clothing, the inhabitants exercise much thrift and industry. They card and spin the wool of their sheep, which they weave into cloth on looms of their own construction. Some of the wool is dyed red or brown from lichens, and black from a mineral clay found in the island : the dye in each case adhering to the wool by a previous application of bark. As I had seen weaving on native looms at Barra on my last year's excursion, there is nothing singular in this system of home manufacture, which is indeed common in all the alpine districts of Northern Europe. It was satisfactory to find in our communication with the inhabitants that all spoke English ; and as all can read, our presents of newspapers were received with a degree of gratification which could not have been experienced in the outer Hebrides. As for Gaelic, nothing of it is known in Orkney or Shetland. We have in these islands got beyond the region of Gaelic, and are amidst the descendants of a Scandinavian people.

I was told there were four slated houses in Foula, but we saw only two, which were chapels—one of them being in connection with the Established Church, and the other maintained by the Congregational Union of Scotland. Except for this Congregational chapel, and the missionary who is deputed as its minister, the island would be poorly off for religious ordinances. According to the Statistical Account of 1798, the parish incumbent was able to visit Foula only once a year ; and the same thing is said in the Account of 1841, with the further remark, that on these annual visits, 'the minister remains in the island two Sabbaths, preaching frequently during the interval.' There are said to be a few members of the Free Church. By a school beneficently planted in the island by the Society for Propagating Christian Knowledge, the children are taught the elementary branches of education.

Measuring three miles in length by one and a half in breadth, Foula is occupied by about two hundred and fifty inhabitants. Depending for subsistence on the catching of fish and the farming of a few acres of land, and dwelling in huts such as I have noticed, their condition, as a stranger might think, is by no means enviable. I am told, however, that they do not experience any serious discomfort. All the families have sheep and cattle more or less in number, and several have saved money, which is placed out at interest. In the social condition of these people, there is not a little to command respect. Using no intoxicating drink, and free from other causes of demoralisation, they are sober, contented, and virtuous. They give trouble to no magistrate, and a breach of the law, I might say an indiscretion, is scarcely known in this simple community. Thinking of all this, one is half inclined to recall a wish to see the islanders in the hands of an emigration agent, to be settled in a country possessing doubtless unbounded material advantages, but associated with innumerable temptations and responsibilities. Latterly several young men have emigrated, and the population is not increasing.

Foula, of course, is owned by a proprietor (Dr Scott of Melby), who draws rents from his tenantry, and is charged with the obligations of a landlord. The annual rental drawn by him is, I believe, £110, paid to a factor who negotiates the purchase of fish from the tenants. Under the auspices of the factor, a store for the sale of articles is established at a hamlet, known as Hametown, situated on the shore, about a mile east from where we landed. At this store there is always a good supply of oatmeal, flour, tea, sugar, tobacco, and other articles, which, in the absence of money-circulation, are given in barter for fish, hosiery, eggs, or anything else of exchangeable value. The women bring

 these articles in a species of creel made of woven straw, which they carry on their backs by means of a band across the breast. A creel or basket of this kind, called a *casie*, seems to be a very common vehicle for the conveying of commodities. At Lerwick, I saw it employed in the transit of peat. With

A Shetland Casie.

her loaded casie, the Foula housewife proceeds to make her market at the store, where, for so much tea and sugar, she will pay down so many eggs, and in like manner will give exchanges for soap, salt, tobacco, needles, or such other things as she requires. I believe that cattle, wool, fish, and some other merchandise are exported by some of the tenants to Reawick on the mainland of Shetland. A room is reserved at the store to be let to any casual stranger, and that is the only semblance of an inn in Foula. There is no regular communication with the island. The ordinary method of reaching it is by fishing-boats from Walls or Reawick. As regards posts, it is further from London than New Zealand. A letter posted in Edinburgh last October did not reach its destination at Foula till the succeeding March.

An intercourse of an hour with the inhabitants was so effectual in rubbing off their shyness, that a crowd followed us from the scattered clachan we had been visiting to the boat ; and one of their own shallops, rowed by four men, with a boy, a barefooted urchin, in the stern, followed us as a friendly convoy to the ship. They said they had never before seen a steam-vessel, except at a great distance, and did not very well know how it was propelled against wind and tide. To satisfy their curiosity, we invited them on board ; and three of them, with the boy, leaping to the deck, were shewn the wonders of the engine-room and cabins. Conducted to the saloon, they were struck with admiration of its furniture, but, above all, the large mirror, over the marble chimney-piece, filled them with profound astonishment. As a treat to the boy—something, perhaps, for him to remember all his days—he was held up to see himself in the glass; this culminating point in the grotesque scene being provocative of no small degree of merriment. With his pockets stuffed with biscuits, and his hands filled with pictorial newspapers, the little fellow was allowed to escape. Getting into their boat, and respectfully bidding us good-bye, the adventurous party returned to the island to tell of all they had witnessed, and we were left to proceed on our voyage.

To the geologist and lover of picturesque scenery, a sight of Foula would be valueless if its western or more precipitous side were left unvisited. To this side we proceeded, and there a spectacle of marvellous grandeur presented itself. A precipice of red sandstone, disposed in long and finely curving layers, rose in front of us as steep as a wall, to a height, at the loftiest part, of twelve hundred feet, and stretched in varying configuration, for the space of a mile, along the sea-margin. In comparison to this, Noss Head, Sumburgh Head, and Barra Head—all grand and imposing—sink into inferiority. The cliffs of Foula have no match in point of height and extent in the British Islands. It would have enhanced the scene, had the long swelling waves rolled in from the Atlantic in the fury which they frequently demonstrate on this wild coast; but, on the other hand, we had reason to congratulate ourselves on a state of the weather which permitted us to relish the spectacle without any unpleasant drawback. As at the other headlands just mentioned, numerous sea-birds build their nests on the cliffs of Foula. The catching of these animals for the sake of their feathers formed a leading pursuit, which has latterly been abandoned. Eagles also take up their quarters on the cliffs, and would commit serious havoc on the live-stock of the islanders but for the Skua Gull, or Bonxie, as it is called by the islanders—the *Lestris cataractes*, I presume. These gulls, with powerful beak and indomitable courage, attack the eagles, and keep their numbers within bounds. Of these gulls, which may be said to act as a police among the feathered tribes, there are only thirteen pairs on Foula, which is the only place in Shetland where they build their nests, and are now to be found. The proprietor pays one of the islanders to attend to these birds, and to prevent any one destroying them.

Having seen these sublime cliffs, there was nothing further to detain us. The head of the *Pharos* was turned in a south-westerly direction towards the shores of Orkney; and after a straight run, during which no vessel hove in sight, we got safely to our anchorage in Otterswick Bay while it was still good daylight.

CHAPTER V.

WEDNESDAY, *July 31.*—We are in Otterswick Bay, in the island of Sanday, one of the Orkney islands, having the previous day quitted the Shetland group, from which we are now separated by a broad sea, not greatly disturbed by traffic. Early in the morning, while the steam is getting up, I go upon deck to talk to the captain, and to see the nature of the country around. A single glance reveals a different condition of things from what we had seen for the last few days. Setting aside Sumburgh and some other favoured spots, the land in Shetland had a bare, unimproved aspect. Here, with certainly less of the picturesque, I observe lands in apparently the highest state of cultivation—fields, of proper dimensions, enclosed by stone dykes, under a rotation of cropping such as one sees in the Lothians; and in place of the thatched hovels of a poor tenantry, large, well-built farm establishments, amidst which rise tall chimneys, indicative of steam-engines, and the other mechanical appliances of an intelligently conducted husbandry.

That is the picture presented by Sanday, and not by it alone; for in the course of this and the succeeding day, I saw, conclusively, that the Orkney islands are, for the most part, in a remarkable state of agricultural advancement. Why such should be the case would, perhaps, involve the telling of a long story. A soil generally fertile, or, at least, susceptible of improvement by draining and otherwise; also enterprising landlords, and farmers with capital, may be presumed to have much to do with the present state of affairs. But, I believe, the explanation would be incomplete were it not mentioned, that no good was done in Orkney until farming was entirely dissociated from fishing. Wherever the two professions are joined, there you see poverty, and worse than poverty, the degradation of women; for on them is imposed—or rather, I should say, by them is voluntarily assumed—the obligations of field-labour, the digging and carrying of peats, and other drudgeries wholly unbefitting their sex. Another and more significant cause of the change of affairs is said to have been the sudden collapse of the kelp manufacture, which caused proprietors to rely exclusively on agricultural resources. I know of no part of Scotland relying mainly on rural industry that has made such rapid strides in advance as Orkney. Its exports, which amounted to only £39,677 in 1800, had risen to £192,863 in 1866 *—a surprising instance of improvement in a group of islands cut off from the mainland of Scotland by a sea of difficult navigation, and situated hundreds of miles from the centre of commercial enterprise. The whole fact of Orkney improvement speaks volumes for the intelligence, self-reliance, and indomitable industry of its people. A certain section of the United Kingdom that is continually calling out for legislation and for 'something to be done for it,' may take a lesson from this limited and unfavourably situated, also, looking to past events, ill-treated community.

Only in one particular did I notice a resemblance between Shetland and Orkney, and that was the want of trees. Offering a gratifying spectacle of rural wealth, Orkney had still that general deficiency of adornment, which trees and their foliage alone can remedy.

---

* Prefatory chapter to a neat reprint of Barry's *History of the Orkney Islands* (W. Peace, Kirkwall, 1867)—a volume which, in point of editing and mechanical execution, would do no discredit to the metropolis.

Our operations for the day were to consist in the inspection of three light-houses in succession. The first establishment visited was that on the island of North Ronaldshay; the next was the light-house on Start Point, a promontory of the island of Sanday; and the last of all was a recently erected light-house on the small island of Auskerry, which lies at the entrance to Stronsay Firth, and acts as a guide to the Bay of Kirkwall. The inspecting of them proved a tolerably hard day's work ; for the tower of North Ronaldshay is of great height, and the ascent of the long winding stair at Auskerry is scarcely less fatiguing. Thankful that this duty was over, we looked lovingly up the sound to Kirkwall ; and when that port, the capital of Orkney, was reached in the course of the afternoon, the Commissioners felt that they had earned a title to some hours of relaxation. There the town lay in front of us, situated with a northern exposure on a spacious declivity to the water, somewhat in the striking manner of Lerwick, but it was of greater extent, and in the midst of all standing out grandly was seen the ancient cathedral of St Magnus.

All of course are going on shore. ' Boat out,' shouts the captain, and off we all pour ; dinner being commanded at half-past six o'clock, at which one or two guests may possibly be expected to make their appearance. Rounding a handsome new iron jetty, we are landed at the flight of stone steps at the old pier, and are left to ramble about at will. Brief as was my visit to Kirkwall, it was more than usually satisfactory. I was more pleased with it than with any town of its size I had seen for a long time. It is clean, neat, old-fashioned. The narrow streets, paved all over with flagstones, as at Lerwick, are lined with buildings of the style of the seventeenth century, when Scottish domestic architecture was distinguished for its picturesque tastefulness. Instead, therefore, of the bald frontages of the eighteenth century, we find in Kirkwall the tapering crow-stepped gables, the ornamental gateways with heraldic insignia, and the small quadrangular courtyards which characterised the era of the later Stuarts. In these well-preserved specimens of an interesting style of architecture, we see the dwellings of the Orcadian gentry in past times, and yet not altogether past, for till this day the houses I speak of are mostly occupied by a respectable order of families—not degraded by an invasion of paupers from all quarters of the kingdom, as is unhappily the case with the old mansions in Edinburgh. But besides these antique buildings, Kirkwall exhibits traces of modern prosperity and taste, including the erection of a new hotel, the opening of new thoroughfares, and the erection of handsome villas in the neighbourhood.

The first rush of our party was, of course, to the cathedral, an imposing structure of red and light coloured sandstone, founded in honour of St Magnus at the middle of the twelfth, but not finished till the early part of the sixteenth century. The style is rounded and massive. Long in a very bad condition, much has been done at the cost of the government to clear the nave, and repair parts of the structure, which were greatly damaged. But something remains to be effected. The chancel, enclosed with a glass screen, is stuffed with galleries and a crowd of common-place pews, for the accommodation of the parish church—a thing which might surely be amended. At a short distance are the ruins of the Bishop's Palace, and also the open ruin of the palace or castle of Patrick Stewart, Earl of Orkney.

The Bishop's Palace, now greatly dilapidated, is that in which Hacon died, after his defeat at Largs, 1263. The building had probably gone to decay previous to 1540, for when James V. visited Kirkwall that year, he was accommodated in a dwelling within the town occupied by Bishop Marshall. The most prominent part of the ruin of the Bishop's Palace is a round tower, adjoining the street. The Earl's Palace, almost contiguous, is an elegant and massive structure, two stories in height, with numerous ornamental devices. The lower floor consists of several vaulted apartments, and ascending a broad staircase we reach a fine large banqueting hall with oriel windows, and two lesser apartments—the whole open to the sky, and with floors overgrown with grass. The large lordly hall forms one of the scenes of historical interest which Sir Walter Scott, with marvellous skill, introduces into the novel of the *Pirate;* for he makes the apartment the place of meeting of Cleveland with his frolicsome lieutenant, Jack Bunce. This remarkably elegant structure was still roofed and entire, though going to decay, when seen by Brand in 1700 ; for he speaks of the ceilings as being painted with scriptural devices. The walls are still strong and tolerably perfect, and at a moderate cost the building might be restored to a habitable condition. I am told that a notion has been entertained of restoring the edifice, in order to serve as a suite of county buildings, which are much required. Within the enclosures occupied by these different ruins, some trees have grown up, to shew us that in sheltered situations, and with other favouring circumstances, trees may even be made to thrive in Orkney. I inquired for the old castle of Kirkwall, which was held out by Robert Stewart against the royal forces under the Earl of Caithness, and found that the ruins, which stood on the line of the main street, nearly opposite the cathedral, had

E

been lately removed to make way for a cross thoroughfare and provide a site for the Castle Hotel. An inscription on this new and handsome building points out with great good taste the ancient situation of the castle.

An acquaintance, who visited Kirkwall five-and-forty years ago, mentions to me that on landing, he was somewhat amused by being made the subject of scrutiny all round by a tailor, who wished to see the latest Edinburgh pattern of clothing. This was in the days of sailing-packets, when matters were somewhat rudimental. Since that primitive period, through the regular visits of steamers and a daily post, Orkney may boast of having no need of strangers as pattern-cards, nor of being without a proper knowledge of the outer world generally. The shops of one kind and another in the principal street in Kirkwall exhibit a profusion of articles sufficient for all wants; and with two native newspapers, the place has nothing to complain of as regards the diffusion of intelligence. The daily mail, however, brought across the Pentland Firth by a steamer from Scrabster to Stromness, gives Orkney an incalculable advantage over Shetland; and the same thing may be said as regards roads, of which I had a good example in an excursion to Stennis.

To be quite plain, the possibility of effecting this excursion had been a leading inducement for quitting home, and giving up a fortnight to the business of the Commission. Our ramble through Kirkwall had accordingly another object besides the sight of St Magnus. It was to hire an open carriage and pair of horses, to take a number of us across the country next morning on this important trip. Having adjusted the matter to our satisfaction, we betook ourselves to the steps at the old pier, and were rowed to the

Pharos, taking with us the resident sheriff-substitute, Mr James Robertson, an old friend, whom we persuaded to honour us with his company at dinner.

Thursday, August 1.—This was a great day. While two of the Commissioners and the Secretary remained on board. to proceed with the vessel round by Scapa Flow to Graemsay, a party of five, two being Commissioners—namely, Mr Falshaw, senior bailie of Edinburgh, and myself—set off from the quay in the carriage hired the preceding evening; the arrangement being that we were to be taken on board the *Pharos* at Stromness, opposite Graemsay, at one o'clock in the afternoon.

It was a merry little journey this. We were going to see two of the most remarkable antiquities in Orkney—the Maeshowe and the Standing Stones of Stennis, regarding which volumes have been written, without, I am sorry to say, throwing much light on their history. The truth is. there are numerous memorials of long-past ages, of the origin or meaning of which nobody can say anything satisfactory. In France, England, Scotland, and Ireland there are structural remains which date from a period considerably before the era of written record. We usually speak of the Celts as being the aborigines of these countries; but were they so? That has never been proved. There is. on the contrary, reason for thinking that the Celts were intruders on a more ancient people; and to this early race, of whom all tradition has vanished, we may venture to refer those wonderful circles, such as Stonehenge and Stennis, also those artificial mounds containing vaulted chambers. exemplified in several places in England and Ireland, and at Maeshowe in Orkney. What has considerably mystified the origin of these old structures is, that on many of them have

been found Runic or Norse inscriptions, and also Christian
symbols, of a date not earlier than the middle ages; but
archæologists are now beginning to understand that these
carvings were executed long after the structures were raised,
and by a class of persons who knew as little of their origin
as we do.   Having, two years ago, been bewildered with
the gigantic dimensions of Stonehenge, I was prepared for
the less imposing circle of Stennis; having, candle in hand,
groped my way into a massive underground structure at
Newgrange, on the banks of the Boyne, near Drogheda, it
was not likely I would be greatly astonished at the sight of
Maeshowe.   Though ardently desirous of seeing Stennis and
Maeshowe, I did not, like most of those who accompanied
me, anticipate the pleasure of a new sensation.

Skirting the Bay of Kirkwall on the right, and with
Whiteford Hill, now agriculturally enclosed and improved,
on our left, we drove along a road of singularly good construction; for independently of its commodious width, it is
rendered as nearly level as circumstances admit, by cutting
through the hillocks and filling up the hollows; and it
possesses the additional recommendation of being free of the
abomination of toll-bars.   Turning the high ground on our
left, and with faces directed westward to Stromness, we
reach Maeshowe, at the distance of nine miles from Kirkwall.
It is situated in a heathy spot on our right, and quitting
the carriage, we get at it by crossing a field.   Outwardly,
there is little to be seen—only a circular grassy tumulus, or
barrow, as it is called by antiquaries, measuring 36 feet high,
and about 92 feet in diameter at the base, at which a low
door presents itself.   Made aware of our errand, a girl from
the neighbouring farmhouse arrives with the key of the
door, a couple of candles, and a box of lucifer-matches.   We

have also bits of candles with us; and with the whole lighted, we enter the aperture, crouching as we advance along a passage varying from a width of 2 feet 4 inches at the entrance to 3 feet 4 inches, at the opening into the interior chamber. The height, low at first, expands to 4 feet 8 inches. The passage is formed by slabs of stone,

Maeshowe : Exterior View, from a photograph by Mr Marwick.

above, below, and along the sides. On issuing into the central chamber, our candles at first feebly enable us to comprehend its dimensions. These we at length discover. We are in a vault built of slabs of stone, measuring 15 feet square, except at the corners where there are buttresses. The height is 13 feet. On each of the sides, except that with the entrance, at a height of 3 feet from the floor, there is a square opening to a cell or recess, the largest of which is 7 feet in length by 4 feet 6 inches in breadth. The roof of the vault had originally been constructed with slabs advancing successively layer above layer to the centre; but as a result of recent repairs, when the structure was cleared out and restored to something like its former condition, the roof is now partly composed of arched masonry, with an aperture for ventilation.

As can be easily supposed, this strange subterranean chamber is cold and clammy. The slabs of stone are wet

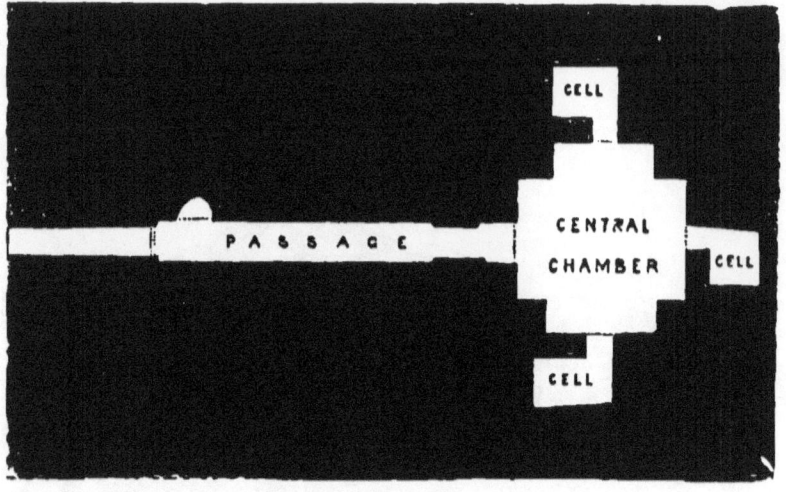

Maeshowe : Ground-plan.

with damp, and nothing induces a protracted stay but the wish to examine certain Runic inscriptions and emblematic or fanciful figures carved on a few of the stones. These carvings were discovered only at the opening and repairing the chamber, an operation undertaken at the instance of Mr James Farrer, M.P., a learned and enthusiastic antiquary. In a privately circulated work on Maeshowe, by Mr Farrer, and also in a work by Mr J. M. Mitchell, the carvings have been explained partly through the assistance of Norwegian scholars. All refer to Vikings and other Scandinavian heroes.

or to transactions in the middle ages. The adjoining cut represents one of these inscriptions. According to Mr Farrer's interpretation, it signifies: 'Molf Kolbainson carved these Runes to Ghaut'—Ghaut being possibly a comrade who fell in battle. Mr Mitchell's translation runs thus : ' Tholfe Kobainsson cut these Runes (on) this cave.' Such is

Runes, interior of Maeshowe.

a pretty fair specimen of the interpretations of the. different inscriptions ; scarcely two persons agreeing in the significa- tion. Several purport to refer to hidden treasure, a circum- stance which throws a degree of ridicule over the whole, for no one carves inscriptions on stones telling the world where money is secretly deposited. Of the emblematic or fanciful figures, nothing can be made. One is a figure of a horse with an animal like an otter in its mouth, a second is a winged dragon, and a third is a worm knot. These figures may represent the names of ships, or may be whimsicalities signifying nothing.

There is nothing in these Runes to explain the origin or use of the structure. We are left to conjecture that it was erected as a sepulchral vault in extremely remote times ; and being opened by Scandinavian rovers, in the hope of discovering hidden treasure, they used it as a resort or hiding-place, and carved the inscriptions which still remain to attest their visits. Obviously, the building and the passage communicating with it were erected on the open plain, and then covered with the earth which forms the tumulus. There is at some distance an environing mound and ditch, still pretty entire.

The whole structure bears a resemblance to the vaulted tumuli in other parts of the British Islands. I observed that at Newgrange the walls are composed of tall blocks set on end; whereas, at Maeshowe, the slabs are built one above another (without mortar), as in an ordinary wall. This general resemblance points to a common origin. We have yet to learn, however, why this part of Orkney should be so rich in memorials of an extreme antiquity. Was it one of the last refuges of the race who constructed Stonehenge? Certainly, at all events, the circles of stone, wherever situated, were the work of a kindred people.

Looking westwards from Maeshowe, we observe, at the distance of a mile and a half, on a heathy tongue of land projected between two lochs, all that remains of the great stone circle of Stennis. In walking thither, we have occasion to pass three slabs stuck on end, and one or two fallen, being what had formed part of a circle of limited radius— the remainder of the group having been, a number of years ago, ruthlessly destroyed, and carted off for building purposes. Quitting these, we pass two detached stones standing gauntly by the wayside; and, according to all accounts, various others have fallen down and been removed. For the disappearance of one stone we may feel a special regret. It was the upright pillar perforated by a circular hole, through which loving couples were wont to join hands when they took the Promise of Odin, as is referred to by Sir Walter Scott, in the *Pirate*. The whole of the detached stones appear to be the relics of a kind of avenue between the lesser and the larger circle. One of these vertical slabs stands at the commencement of a causeway which crosses a channel between the two contiguous lochs, and underneath which the tide is suffered to flow through conduit-like apertures. By this causeway, designated the Bridge of Brogar, we reach the tongue of land on which the circle of Stennis is situated.

Occupying an elevated piece of ground, with an inclination towards us, the circle stands well out, and we at once recognise its general appearance. A few paces up the ascent from the road along the side of the inner loch, bring us to it ; but it is environed by a sunk ditch, that is to be crossed before we get within the circle. I have no difficulty in perceiving that it is inferior in several important particulars to Stonehenge, which, as is well known, comprised two circles, one within the other ; the outer one, consisting of thirty upright blocks, being connected together by squared slabs laid horizontally along the top, so as to form a complete ring. We have no such artistic traces at Stennis. The stones are unshapely slabs, stuck in the ground just as they had been excavated from the quarry, and there has been no connecting ring of stones around the top of the circle. Comparatively inferior as it may be, the circle of Stennis is nevertheless a remarkably interesting relic of antiquity ; it may be fairly styled the Stonehenge of Scotland, and is exceedingly worthy of a visit.

The circle, which has a diameter of 366 feet, occupies a slope with an inclination to the east ; one side being 6 or 7 feet lower than the other. Originally, as is thought, there had been sixty stones in the circle. In the course of time, a number have been improperly taken away. At present, there are sixteen standing, and about as many lying on the ground. As it would be an easy matter to have these raised and stuck in their former positions, I suggested to Mr Falshaw that we should there and then initiate a public subscription to have the fallen stones raised and set in their places, and also to set securely upright those which were leaning over; a suggestion which instantly met with approval. Mr Marwick, who was with us, undertook to bring the subject before the Council of the Society of Scottish Antiquaries, under whose auspices the work should be undertaken, after procuring the concurrence of the proprietor, Mr Balfour of Balfour and Trenabie. In carrying out this moderate restoration, it would be proper to clear out the exterior fosse, which is partially grown up, and likewise to repair some tumuli in the vicinity, that have been left in an odiously defaced condition by explorers.

On our way back to the carriage, the bailie asked how old I thought the circle was, and what was the purpose of its erection. ' These,' I said, ' are very puzzling questions : if I ventured to say that circles of that kind are three thousand years old, I would probably be within the truth as to their antiquity; the purposes of their construction were most likely some kind of pagan religious rites, but after such rites were abandoned, the circles may still have been used as places of public assemblage.' This, I believe, is the sum and substance of all that can be reasonably said about the circles of Stonehenge, Stennis, Callernish in Lewis, or any similar monument. If they defy our investigation, they at least invite a rational curiosity, and, as relics of long by-past ages, mutely appeal to us for protection.

From the point where the cross-road to Stennis joins the main thoroughfare, the distance is about five miles to Stromness, the approach to which, across a ridge of high ground, affords a comprehensive view of the lofty island of Hoy, with the intermediate low island of Graemsay. Stromness, a long straggling town, situated on a well-sheltered bay, had little to interest us. Shortly after we had taken a walk through the place, the *Pharos* made its appearance in the bay, and making a signal from a slip of quay, a boat was put out to take us on board. With some regret, we now parted with Mr Marwick, who was left to return by the carriage to Kirkwall, where he designed to remain for a few days.

The bay opposite Stromness is an offshoot of the Sound of Hoy, by which, after an inspection of two light-houses on Graemsay, the vessel pursued its way into the Pentland Firth. I regretted that time and circumstances would not permit our landing on the island of Hoy, the most lofty of the Orkneys, and noted for containing the 'Dwarfie Stone,' a detached block of sandstone, in which, according to Norse superstitious legend, a dwarfish demon, or Trow, had excavated two small apartments as a residence. Leaving this local wonder unvisited, we entered the Pentland Firth in calm and sunshine, which enabled us to see with advantage the Old Man of Hoy. This is a tall natural column of red sandstone, detached from the cliff by the action of the sea, and standing well out on the rocky shore. Formerly, it was higher than it is now, and bore that resemblance to the human figure, by which it procured its present designation. Even lessened in dimensions, the column is not unlike a petrified giant, stationed as a sort of out-sentinel of the Orkneys, and we see it for a great distance in crossing the Firth to the coast of Caithness. Fortunately for us, the weather had now become exceedingly pleasant, and still more fortunate, the contending tides of the Firth were at rest. Early in the evening, we arrived safely at Scrabster in the Bay of Thurso.

Brought back to the mainland of Scotland, I may cease the scribbling of these random notes. Only a few words remain to be added. On Friday, August 2, the Commissioners visited the light-house on Holburn Head, and then proceeded on their voyage eastward through the Pentland Firth, stopping first at Dunnet Head, a conspicuous promontory, with a light-house situated on the cliff at the distance of a mile and a half from the landing-place. Thence, the *Pharos* pursued its way, passing the hamlet of Houna and the adjoining bare grassy knoll popularly known as John o' Groat's House, where no house, as far as can be distinguishable, ever existed. That there may have been a personage of inventive faculties styled John o' Groat is probable enough, for the patronymic belongs to the district; but the story of this northern genius having built an octagonal house with eight doors, possessing a table with eight sides, so as to lay any question of precedency among eight family claimants, is too like the fable of the Knights of the Round Table to be anything else than a legendary myth.

Shooting past this spot, the *Pharos* stopped for a short time at the rocky islets called the Pentland Skerries. Here, at the entrance to the Firth from the east, the tide was exceedingly turbulent; boiling up furiously in consequence of having to force its way between the islands which obstruct the channel. The vessel, however, was able to maintain its course. Such is not always the case. The captain informed me that on one occasion the *Pharos* was kept three hours in one spot, for the impetus of ten miles an hour given by the paddles was just equal to the retarding force of the current. Sometimes, in spite of all that mariners can do, their ships are carried out of their course by the currents, and dashed to pieces on the coast. At one of our landing-places some few remains of one of these unhappily wrecked vessels were lying on the shore. The Commissioners have done what is in their power to avert such catastrophes and give confidence to those who have to navigate this wild and uncertain sea. They have placed a light-house on each of the following prominent places—the Pentland Skerries, Dunnet Head, Holburn Head near Scrabster, and Cape Wrath. A noble object has been nobly effected. I could not help contrasting the present with the past method of crossing this dangerous Firth. In former times the traveller had to be ferried in boats from island to island, and often from stress of weather was detained for days at the small inn at Houna. Now, there is a steamer carrying the mails, which courageously crosses daily between Scrabster and Stromness—keeping up that communication which is so advantageous to the Orcadians. The easiest way of getting to Orkney from the south is, of course, to proceed by one of the well-appointed steamers from Granton; but those who have a fancy to see mail-coaches with the red-coated guards of the olden time, may take the route for Thurso and Scrabster through Sutherlandshire and Caithness; for there they still flourish in a style which will comfort all, who hating hurry, cherish a detestation of railways. Yet, travellers with old-fashioned tastes had better be quick: a railway to Thurso is threatened.

On Saturday, August 3, stopping at several light-houses *en route*, and passing through fleets of Wick fishing-boats, the vessel reached Cromarty Firth, where it lay opposite the small and very dull town of Cromarty all Sunday. On Monday, it proceeded to Inverness, where the second voyage, with other Commissioners, was to commence. Pressed by public duties, I returned by railway from Invergordon, on the Cromarty Firth, and reached home on Monday afternoon; thus concluding My Second Year's Holiday, of which I shall ever retain as pleasant recollections as of the first— more particularly retaining a vivid remembrance of the solitary isle of Foula, and the marvellous grandeur of its precipices.

Island of Foula.

Edinburgh: Printed by W. and R. Chambers.